Tête-bêche (n)
A book split into two parts printed back-to-back and head-to-foot.
Etymology: French *lit.* 'head-to-foot'.

I have recently bought a *tête-bêche*. It is a beguiling thing. Two stories are printed in mutual inversion. One reads the first, then turns the book over and reads the other. These tales are intertwined and parasitic. Beguiling and, I think, a little strange too.

Letter from COUNT HORACE MANN,
20 March 1819

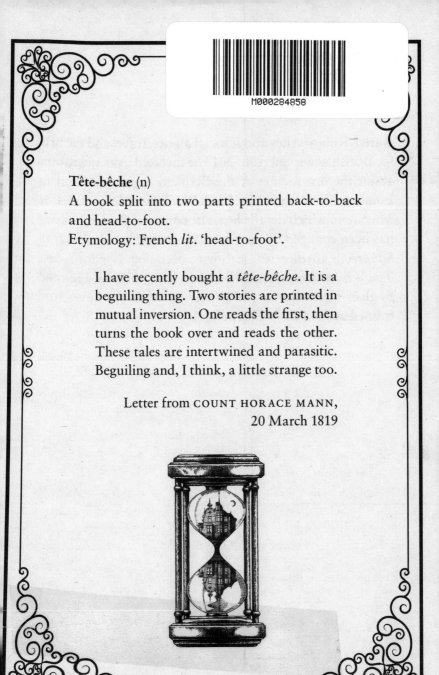

Gareth Rubin writes about social affairs, travel and the arts for British newspapers. In 2013 he directed a documentary about therapeutic art at the Bethlem Royal Hospital in London ('Bedlam'). His books include *The Great Cat Massacre*, which details how the course of British history has been changed by people making mistakes; *Liberation Square*, a thriller set in Soviet-occupied London; and *The Winter Agent*, a thriller set in Paris in 1944. He read English Literature at the University of St Andrews and trained at East 15 Acting School.

The TURNGLASS

GARETH RUBIN

**SIMON &
SCHUSTER**

London · New York · Sydney · Toronto · New Delhi

First published in Great Britain by Simon & Schuster UK Ltd, 2023
This paperback edition first published 2024

Copyright © Gareth Rubin, 2023

The right of Gareth Rubin to be identified as author
of this work has been asserted in accordance with the
Copyright, Designs and Patents Act, 1988.

1 3 5 7 9 10 8 6 4 2

Simon & Schuster UK Ltd
1st Floor
222 Gray's Inn Road
London WC1X 8HB

Simon & Schuster: Celebrating 100 Years of Publishing in 2024

Simon & Schuster Australia, Sydney
Simon & Schuster India, New Delhi

www.simonandschuster.co.uk
www.simonandschuster.com.au
www.simonandschuster.co.in

A CIP catalogue record for this book
is available from the British Library

Paperback ISBN: 978-1-3985-1452-2
eBook ISBN: 978-1-3985-1451-5
Audio ISBN: 978-1-3985-2298-5

Typeset in Sabon by M Rules

Printed and Bound in the UK using 100% Renewable
Electricity at CPI Group (UK) Ltd

MIX
Paper | Supporting
responsible forestry
FSC
www.fsc.org   FSC® C171272

For Phoebe

The TURNGLASS

Wilt thou be gone? It is not yet near day:
It was the nightingale, and not the lark,
That pierced the fearful hollow of thine ear;
Nightly she sings on yon pomegranate-tree:
Believe me, love, it was the nightingale.

Juliet, *Romeo and Juliet*, ACT III SCENE V

Chapter 1

London, 1881

Simeon Lee's grey eyes were visible above a kerchief he had tied to keep out the stench of cholera. It was the odour of bodies rotting in doss-houses and mortuaries.

'The King's come knocking,' he muttered.

'Can't we call it something else?' implored his friend Graham, who had a damp scarf bound over his nose and mouth. 'I don't like that name. It implies we owe it something. We don't.'

'And yet it's going to collect.'

'Do you think there will be another epidemic?'

'I hope not.' No, he hoped this was just a local outbreak of the disease.

The two, who had spent years training together for a career healing the sick and reassuring the healthy, walked on through Grub Street, deep in the ancient Roman heart of the city of London. The buildings in the thoroughfare were given over to the print trade – journals and periodicals cataloguing the daily intrigues, pleasures and sadnesses of life. The gutter along the middle of the lane ran with ink.

Simeon cast aside his face covering as they reached their shared lodging. 'We need to find its weak point,' he said. He thought of the disease in animal terms, like a rabid dog. Too small for the eye to see, and yet the bacterium was strong enough to drag waves of men, women and children to their graves. An insidious little murderer. 'Every disease has a weak point.'

Dr Simeon Lee had long, slim features and a long, slim frame that rose lithely up the stairs to their rooms – their garret, in truth – above a print shop whose presses banged without stop around the clock. The place suited him, however, because he could work when most others rested. And it was cheap. Very cheap. After months when his research had stalled due to a lack of money, he needed to save every penny he could.

'It's there, I can feel it's there,' he continued without missing a beat. 'Damn it, we've been able to protect against smallpox for a century. Why not cholera?' He stared out of the grimy tilted window. The sharp darkness of a December smog stared back at him.

'So you have said, once or twice. You're getting a bit

obsessive.' Graham hesitated. 'You know, you're not making yourself too popular at the hospital.'

'You astonish me.' He did not care a cuss what the ancient bewhiskered creatures who ran the King's College Hospital thought of him. Let them work in the tenements and rookeries around St Giles and they might see things differently.

His friend shrugged in dismissal. 'How do you intend to find your miracle cure?'

'How?' He nearly laughed at the question. 'With money. I need money. I need the Macintosh grant.' He undid his tie and dropped onto the fire-damaged settle they had rescued from a pavement in Marylebone. 'Meanwhile, they fall in their houses like it's the Black Death.' He swivelled on the scorched seat, trying to get comfortable. 'A poor man in this street has less chance of making it to the age of thirty than I have of being knighted. Good God, if Robertson and the others would just listen, we could do something about it!' His friend left the air unbroken as Simeon got into his stride, railing against the faculty of the King's College school of medicine who had time and time again demonstrated their utter inability to entertain a single new idea. 'Time and money. That's all it takes to find a cure. Enough time and enough money.'

His anger was born of frustration. Few things could rile him so much as the prospect of his entire body of three years' work growing dusty on his desk. Every month, the grants board of the medical school hummed and hahed over his proposals, and more men, women and children succumbed to the disease.

'Think you'll get it?'

'It's between me and Edwin Grover. Wants it for his stuff on analgesia.'

'He's bright.'

'On paper, yes. In practical terms, he's a cretin. It's all too theoretical. No thought as to how you would actually get a needle in the arm of a seamstress.' He rapped his knuckles on the table in irritation. Grover spent his days in a set of rooms on the upper floor of a rather fine house on Soho Square. He rarely left them. He had no need. No interest, probably.

'What if you don't get it?'

'Then, my friend, I will be out sweeping the street for ha'pennies.' He tugged his forelock.

'Sounds frosty.'

'No doubt it is.'

Graham cleared his throat. 'What about that job in Essex? It would pay.'

Simeon raised his eyebrows in surprise. 'God, I had forgotten all about that.' It had left Simeon's mind almost as soon as he had laid the telegram aside the day before.

'Your uncle, correct?'

'Not quite. My father's cousin.'

'Well, it's a paying job.'

That was true, but it was not an enticing one. 'Ministering to a country parson who has convinced himself he's at death's door even though he's probably fit enough to go ten rounds in the ring with Daniel Mendoza.'

'Simeon, you *need* the cash.'

He brooded. There was absolutely no doubting that point. But he felt like a cheap hireling, treating a man who probably needed no more medical prescription than 'cut down on the port and take a brisk walk from time to time'. And yet the money could restart his progress towards a cure.

'It is an option,' he conceded. 'Though God knows how much I can shake out of him. A country parson isn't exactly rolling in paper.'

'True. Is he at least a pleasant chap?'

Simeon shrugged. 'No doubt one of these quiet old priests who spend all their time reading treatises about Bishop Ussher's calculation that the world is six millennia old.'

'Well, it could be worse. Is it just him in the house?'

'Ah. Well.' Simeon chuckled to himself. 'That is where it does become rather . . . intriguing.'

'How so?'

'It's the family scandal.'

'Scandal? Go on.'

'I don't even know half of it myself – my father wouldn't tell me the details. I believe the parson's brother was killed by his wife in strange circumstances. One of them was mad, I think. I should find out. True, true, a piquant history might be some respite from the boredom of the job. But no, I put my trust in Providence that the Macintosh board will come through first.'

The following afternoon, Simeon sat on a hard, well-polished bench outside a committee room in King's

College. Edwin Grover, primly dressed, sat on an identical bench opposite.

'Still on cholera, are you?' Grover asked.

'Yes. Still on it.'

Grover had no more questions.

An elderly porter creaked out of the committee room. 'Dr Grover? Will you come this way?'

Grover followed him in. The door closed with a bang that echoed up the hall.

It was an hour before he emerged, looking pleased with himself. Simeon swore under his breath at the sight; then it was his turn.

He entered, sat on a wooden chair before a panel of five men and laid out his plans to cure one of the greatest ills of the age.

'Dr Lee. We have been reviewing your application and supporting documents,' one informed him morosely. 'One question kept arising in our minds.'

'What question, sir?'

'What evidence do we have that you will actually get anywhere?'

It was not a friendly question. 'Can you be more specific?'

'Your record seems,' he glanced down at a file, '*incon-sequential*. Nothing, we understand, has, in fact, come out of it.'

'I don't believe that—'

'Unlike, say, another candidate's record that shows two papers published in the *Lancet* alone.' Somewhere in the walls, the water pipes banged and hooted with trapped air.

'I have the utmost respect for academic publishing—'

'Whereas all we can see from your work is a series of requests for more funding.'

Simeon gritted his teeth before answering. 'I believe the return will be worth the capital, sir.'

'But what return? And how much capital?'

'I think three hundred pounds would—'

'Three hundred pounds? For a disease now confined to the slums?' There were murmurings of agreement from the rest of the panel. 'It is what those who live in such places are used to. They are born into it. They will live their lives in it.'

'And if you spent as much time in their company as I have, you would know that many of them are better off *not* living in it.'

'Your meaning?' the elderly doctor asked.

'My meaning, sir, is that I can't tell you the number of children younger than five years of age that I have seen who were condemned to nothing more than a short, pain-filled life. At times it has been tempting to cut their lives short then and there rather than watch their inevitable decline.'

'Well, that is between you and God. Here, we are concerned with your application for a grant.'

'Of course. I apologize for becoming distracted. To answer your precise question: we have been unable to identify vaccine-worthy material from human sources. My contention is that non-human animals may possibly produce the material we need. For example, if we expose our closest relatives, gorillas, to the disease, and we extract

11

their blood, it is possible that consanguination may provide protection against the germ.'

'So now he wants us all swinging from trees,' muttered one of the men.

When Simeon arrived back in his rooms, there was an open bottle of dark wine on the trunk they used as a table. He drained its dregs, glanced at his friend gently snoring in his bed and looked out the window. The street was quiet as the grave.

He noticed then that the bottle had been resting on something: a telegram. The day before, he had sent a cable to his father, asking for details of the murderous events involving his relatives in Essex two years earlier that had set vicious tongues wagging. The reply had been swift. 'Your duties are purely medical. Do them and no more. I understand that nefarious crimes were suspected even before the violence took place. It is no surprise to me. Turnglass House has always had something corrupt and malign about it. Leave it to God and the law.'

Simeon could not help but remark on the fact that his father – not usually a man for flights of poetic fancy – had said it was the house itself that had 'something corrupt and malign' about it, rather than the household. That was curious.

Simeon had never known the distant branch of the family who resided at Turnglass House. He had grown up hundreds of miles to the north, among the stone streets of York, a sole surviving child raised by parents with only a passing interest in him, and sent away for his education at the age of ten. His father, a solicitor with a dusty practice tending to the needs of dusty aristocrats, accepted medicine as a reasonable profession, although he supposed his mother would probably have preferred if Simeon had set his cap at a more fashionable business in Harley Street. Her subsequent disapproval of a career in researching and combating infectious diseases did nothing to slake her son's thirst for it.

So it's Essex then, he thought to himself.

The island of Ray lies in the salt marshes on the edge of the Essex coast. It is, or is not, an island depending on the tide – resting, as it does, between the open mouths of the Colne and Blackwater estuaries. At high tide it is quite cut off, and the sole house that resides on it feels adrift and isolated. The sea that pours in between the mainland and Ray is topped by a carpet of tangling Sargasso weed, like the fingers of so many drowned men. The weed drifts in its own time through the creeks of the estuary, up to the village of Peldon on the mainland, where the pond outside the Peldon Rose inn has long been a store locker for those supplementing their incomes as oyster fishermen with sales of brandy and tobacco that have been brought from the Continent without paying the ruinous excise duty. The bottom of the pond is wooden and can be lifted to drain away the water, revealing the tar-crusted barrels secreted therein. These barrels supply all the inns of Colchester with wine and all the haberdashers with lace.

Indeed, barely a penny of excise is collected in Essex, even though a quarter of the nation's excisable goods are imported through that county. And don't imagine that the excise men are unaware of the trade, but since twenty-two of their number were found in a boat one morning some years back with their throats slashed, their friends have been loath to interrupt the local tradesmen.

Beside Ray sits the neighbouring island of Mersea, which is ten times Ray's size and home to fifty-odd homes and a shingle beach known as the Hard. Golden samphire and purple sea lavender decorate both islands, which have a gravel base packed together with clay that attracts wading and floating birds, such as oystercatchers and shelduck.

Yet human visitors to these islands must take care.

At low tide, a narrow causeway from the mainland, the Strood, is revealed by the departing brine. It runs to Ray, across the mile-wide island and then on to Mersea. But anyone who walks it must ensure they have checked the tidal calendar. The danger is not just being marooned on Ray, with its obscure house, but more that anyone caught on the Strood itself as the saltwater rises risks being claimed by the Sargasso weed. Almost every year since the Romans first populated Ray, at least one man or woman has become entwined in that weed. They float there still, making no sound, no complaint, their hands slowly joining.

Simeon could smell sea lavender on the wind as a pony trap set him down outside the Peldon Rose. The driver had laughingly boasted of the local less-than-legal industry on the way, and Simeon happened to peer into the pond but saw only murky saltwater. The very air tasted of salt, though. It burned a little at the back of his throat, and he tried swallowing two or three times to get rid of it before telling himself he would soon get used to the sensation as part of the landscape.

'Good afternoon, sir,' he heard. The publican, a wiry fellow with huge side-whiskers, was standing in the doorway puffing a long pipe. 'Are ye comin' in?'

'I am, and glad for it,' Simeon replied happily, hefting his travelling bag onto his shoulder and carrying his black leather medical bag in his remaining hand.

'Right then. Ye'll be wantin' somethin' to eat an' a jug-a beer, I shouldn' wonder.'

'That sounds very fine.' He looked over the building. It was a wide, single-storey country inn whitewashed to a dull grey in the winter dun. He was hungry and the prospect of hot food had nourished him for the hour-long ride from Colchester station on his way to see and treat the parson of the parish, Oliver Hawes – Dr Hawes, in fact, that gentleman being a Doctor of Divinity.

'In ye come, then, lad.'

He gladly accepted.

The tap room was populated with seven or eight fellows wearing the clothes of fishermen. Every one was smoking a long, thin white pipe, identical to the landlord's. Simeon wondered if they could somehow tell their own from their friends'. Three women had called in too, forming a trio of Fates in the corner, silently examining him.

'Come on in, lad,' the landlord reiterated. 'Warm

welcome always a' the Rose. Put yer bag down. Tha's it. Jenny! Jenny! Some bread an' twelve – no, sixteen oysters. He looks a hungry one. Sharpish, girl.' He made no attempt to ask if the order met his new patron's needs. Within seconds, Jenny, a girl of about ten years, appeared with bread and a mass of oysters. The landlord handed over a jug of small beer and motioned for Simeon to eat standing at the bar. The whole inn was waiting for him to start eating or announce his business, it seemed. He chose to begin with the food. But if he had been expecting conversation to resume as he ate, he was mistaken. The air remained still, apart from the sound of him, or one other, drinking back ale. Ten minutes later, he had finished his meal.

'Tha'll be four shillings, three pence an' one story,' the landlord informed him.

Simeon chuckled. 'And what story would that be?'

'To tell us all wha' ye're doing here.'

It seemed perfectly friendly, rather than some sort of warning, so Simeon had no compunction regarding a reply. 'I'm a doctor. I'm on my way to look after a relative of mine.'

'Who's tha', then?'

Simeon wondered how they addressed or referred to his almost-uncle. 'Dr Hawes.'

'Parson Hawes!' The landlord's eyebrows shot up and there was a low rumbling in the room. 'Ye're his relative.'

'My father is his cousin.'

'Indeed? Never thought of the parson's family as bein' from anywheres bu' here.'

'I've never actually met him, myself.'

'No, well, if ye're no' from Mersea or Peldon, ye'll no' be doin' so. I heard he was a-sick.' There was a general muttering, but the landlord was clearly the spokesman for them all.

'I'll see him tonight and find out.'

The landlord was concerned. 'Wait 'til the mornin'. Tide's comin' in.'

'Thank you, really,' Simeon replied. 'But I must be going tonight. Dr Hawes is expecting me.'

'Morty, will you take him?' the publican asked one of the knot of men who were making no bones about listening to the conversation.

'I'm the ferryman,' Morty volunteered. He was over sixty and small, but fit as a man who rows in the creeks and seas around Essex must be. 'Ferryman, me.'

'You look a good one.'

'But I'm off home now. Me fire.'

'Is the Strood safe now?' the landlord asked.

'Prob'ly. Won' be running on, bu' he'll get 'cross.'

'Well, that sounds fine to me,' Simeon said. He wanted to get on. 'Will you point me on the way?'

The full population of the inn glanced out the window. There was no rain, but it was past six o'clock and fully winter-dark.

'Ye'll need a lamp,' said the landlord, sounding uncertain that a youngster from the city – probably London – would even know to bring such a thing.

'I have one.'

'Wadin' boots?'

17

'I didn't know I needed them. I'll cope.' He looked down at his leather ankle boots. Well, they had seen better days anyway.

'See how ye get on, then. Straigh' down tha' way. The road becomes the Strood. Ye can't get the wrong place once ye're on Ray. Turnglass House's the only one on the island.'

He was satisfied. 'It's a strange name. How did the place come by it?'

'Look a' the weather vane as ye come in. Ye'll see.' The publican hesitated a little, as if deciding whether to broach a difficult subject. 'No' a bad old stick, Parson Hawes. A bit funny a' times. Bu' he's been good to his sister-in-law after ... well, ye know.' He seemed to be probing to see exactly what Simeon did know.

The family scandal. These people most assuredly knew more about it than he did. It would be worth talking, he thought.

'Yes, I know she killed his brother.'

The landlord looked a little relieved to discover that. 'Righ' well. Good an' tha'. Wouldn' wan' it to be a shock t' hear.'

'It isn't.' His father had given him the bald details, but had been vague about precisely how Florence had killed her husband, James, brother to Oliver. 'But I'm in the dark about exactly what happened.'

'In the dark, eh?' He sounded a little sceptical and mulled his response. 'Ask Morty.'

Morty glared at Simeon. 'So, you don' know, then?'

'Not really, no.'

Morty shrugged. 'Well, 's your family. Your business.' Odd to think that the man was right – it was his business, even though he had never met any of the people concerned. Family, he thought, could be a well of strange connections. 'I took the body – yer uncle James or whate'er-ye-calls-'im – away from the house. Terrible state 'e were in.' Simeon felt a curiosity, both professional and human. 'Puffed-up face. Yellow. The bad'd set in.' He paused. '*Infaction* ye calls it, lad.' He pronounced the word carefully.

'What infection? What happened?'

Morty shrugged as if rehearsing a tale everyone knew. 'She gashed his face. Threw a decanter 'gainst it an' the glass smashed. Bad set in. Turned his flesh black here, yellow there.' He pointed to his own cheek and jaw. 'All puffed up like a pig.'

So Florence had cut James's face deeply enough for blood poisoning to kill him. It must have been quite an assault.

'He were a pretty one afore tha',' one of the three Fates called over. 'Prize o' the county.'

'Why did she do it?' Simeon asked. It was a prurient interest, but everyone else knew, so why shouldn't he?

Morty shook his head mournfully. 'Never asked. Bad thin' to happen here. Don' wan' go too low inta it. I jus' put the coffin in the boat, rowed up t' Virley and carried him to St Mary's. He's six feet under now. Go an' ask him any questions ye have.'

'Morty,' the Fate admonished him.

'Well.' He supped some of his drink ruminatively. There

was a pause as they all joined him. 'Ye know where Mrs Florence is now?'

'No.'

Morty glanced at each of his friends in turn. They returned his heavy look. 'Ye will do soon.'

Chapter 2

The words rang in Simeon's ears as he thanked all for their advice and paid his bill. He felt the sting of the salt at the back of his throat again as he stepped outside and set off once more, tramping the single road that would become the Strood. With the inn behind him, he felt quite alone under the night sky and he enjoyed the brief solitude.

The ground became soft, warning of a marsh, and soon the turf beside the path turned to watery mush, lights from the Rose flickering on its black surface. They seemed like signals from lighthouses to him, flitting back and forth. Then he was on the Strood proper. It was just wide enough for a man to pass along and at its end he made out a broad black mass that bore no flickering reflections: Ray, where his relation awaited him.

Each foot he set down seemed to press lower in the mud. The glittering, glassy water either side of the causeway mocked his laborious progress, and his heels, then his feet and then his ankles sank in. He began to worry that his knees would go in too and that he would be held there until the tide rose above his shoulders. But he chose to trust Morty's assessment that the path was solid enough – just – and to power on. And little by little the way became firmer, until he was on solid land.

Ray, the island that came and went with the tides.

He turned up the flame on his oil lamp and the beam raked the ground for a good distance. He had bought it from a ship's chandler who had assured him it was as strong a light as he would find anywhere, strong enough for ships to find each other a mile away.

It was a bleak place that the light revealed. Deathly so. *Whyever did anyone settle here?* he wondered.

He looked up. A dim prickle of stars was scattered across the sky; but there was a void on the horizon where they were blotted out, where something black and wide loomed up from the waterlogged ground. Turnglass House, the only building on Ray.

A single bright window near its tip was the only sign of habitation.

Coming closer and raking his strong lamp beam over it, Simeon found that the house was three storeys high and wide as a London villa. Beside it stood what looked like a small stable block. A spacious home for a country curate, although even on the brightest spring day the vista must have been a dreary one.

Turnglass House. He thought of the publican's instruction to look at the weather vane in order to understand the name. Peering up to the roof and angling the ship's lantern as best he could, he saw an unusual vane indeed. It was shaped like an hourglass, with a stream of sand cascading from one bulb to the other; but rather than being constructed of metal, the vane was made entirely from glass, and it glinted in the beam. It had to be lead crystal to withstand the wind and rain with which it was constantly buffeted. As he watched, the vane spun languidly, with a whine. The wind must have been changing.

Reaching the house, Simeon found an old-fashioned bell-pull protruding from the brickwork. He tugged it hard, to be answered by a tolling inside, then footsteps and the drawing back of bolts. *Why lock your door on Ray?* he wondered. *Who would come uninvited?*

'Dr Lee?' A cheery, buxom housekeeper was standing aside and he could feel warmth blasting out from the wide hallway.

'Yes.'

'Won't you come in, sir?' He gladly complied.

The house seemed to have been decorated a hundred years earlier. Busts of long-dead poets lined one wall, and a large oil painting of men on a hunt was set above the staircase. The most striking picture, however, was a portrait over the fireplace that showed a very handsome woman with rich brown hair, standing before a glittering house.

'I'm Tabbers, sir. Eliza Tabbers.'

Simeon set down his carryall. 'Are there any other servants here?'

'Yes. There's Cain – Peter Cain. He's the footman, gardener, what you will. We both live out, sir. On Mersea. I come just after dawn to light the fires and I normally leave around seven. Cain's in from eight until five.'

Yes, it would be hard to attract many to live in at a place such as this – just a mile from the nearest village, and yet remote and cut off at the sea's will.

He handed her his overcoat. She placed it in a press beside a table, upon which a jumble of lamps and rusted iron keys resided. 'Would you please take me to Dr Hawes?'

'Right away.'

She led him up the stairs and along a corridor where every surface was covered in rugs, drapes or wall hangings. It all added to a peculiar atmosphere where the air hung without motion and every tread was thick and noiseless. The upper floor, he found, sported three doors off a long corridor, each padded in coloured leather: green, red, blue. Two more at the end were plain wood.

They stopped at the green one, and the housekeeper tapped: three times softly, then three times hard. She was answered by a painful groan from within. At that sign, she showed Simeon in.

It was an extraordinary sight that met him. A church-at-night darkness was pierced by fingers of light from a partly shuttered oil lamp on an octagonal table in the centre of the room. There were gas lamps on the wall, but they were unlit. Instead, the cobweb of beams from the brass table showed Simeon that he was in a library – but one quite different from any he had seen in even the few grand houses that had admitted him.

It rose two complete storeys, almost to the roof of the house, with a row of windows on each storey. Ladders around the room gave access to the books that lined every wall from bottom to top. He realized that the staircase he had climbed only came to the first floor of the house, so it must have been built this way with a cliff-like upper level. It would be heaven for bibliophiles, hell for those who loathed the written word.

Within the room were the silhouettes of reading desks and tables with piles of books. Deep seats had been chosen as platforms for consuming the pages. They were arranged in a sort of ring, and in the centre of it all was a sopha, on which a thin, balding man in his forties had fallen back to snoozing, with the octagonal table and its lamp by his side. The far end of the room was in full shadow, though a flickering reflection of the lamp, like the lights on the dark water outside, suggested a wide panel of glass there.

'Dr Hawes,' the housekeeper hemmed.

Slowly, the man's eyes peeled open behind thick square spectacles. 'Hello? Oh,' the older man's voice wobbled. 'Oh, you must be Winston's boy.'

'I am, sir.'

'Oh, I am glad you came. So glad. Come, come.' He had a kindly tone and tried to beckon Simeon to him, but his hand gave up halfway through the motion.

Simeon approached and offered his palm. The patient

gently gripped and shook it. 'Shall I begin by examining you, sir?' Simeon asked, curious as to what he might find by way of disease or hypochondriasis. 'We may speak as I do so.'

'Examine me? Oh, yes, yes. Of course.'

'May I turn on the gaslights?'

'I am sorry, I find their light quite painfully harsh. I prefer the oil lamp.'

'Of course.' The servant withdrew as Simeon opened his medical bag to take out his stethoscope. 'Now, would you please tell me what the problem is?'

'I, oh, I fear I may be dying,' the parson whispered. 'My heart, you know, and I have such sweats and pains. All over. Pains in my joints, in my organs. My head. And my teeth chatter so. But then I have always been cold.'

Simeon thought the house was warm. There was no fire in the grate, so it must have been one of the systems for wafting hot air through vents throughout the building. 'I shall listen to your heart, then I will take a history,' he explained. The patient duly opened his shirt. Confounding Simeon's expectations of an imaginary illness, that muscle was, in fact, anything but healthy. For a few seconds it would gallop, then flutter and then thud deeply. *Not good*, he thought to himself. 'And when did this begin?'

'Oh, now let me think. Yes, it was Thursday. I am usually strong, despite the chills I feel. But as soon as I woke, I felt a pounding in my head. I took to bed, thinking it was merely an unusually bad chill. But today I am far worse – the pains wrack me and I cannot stand or sleep.'

That was five days of sickness. It certainly seemed

worse than a common infection. If they had been in the city, Simeon would have immediately pointed to King Cholera. But out on the sparsely populated coast it was practically unheard of. Malaria? The ground was marshy, but that disease had been eradicated long ago in these parts.

'Have you eaten anything unusual? Perhaps under-cooked meat?'

'No. Indeed, I eat little meat. I find it excites the blood too much.'

'I see. Could your housekeeper have prepared some unusual mushrooms for you, perhaps?'

'None. Simple bread, cheese, occasional fish or mutton, common vegetables. That is all. And Mrs Tabbers and Cain eat the same dishes at the same time – our household is small, there is little point preparing separate meals.'

'Do you take alcohol?'

The parson looked a little sheepish. 'I usually have a drop of brandy as a nightcap, but have not had the stomach for it since I first became ill.' He waved to a small barrel in a corner of the room. A silver ladle lay beside it, ready to scoop out the drink. It seemed that in these parts, where the excise men feared to tread, even the parsons drank from barrels.

'I think it best to stay away from alcohol for now,' Simeon said. 'So no more nightcaps.' A sound – a slight creaking – made his head turn towards the gloomy end of the room.

'If you say so.'

Simeon went through every potential cause of the

curate's illness that he could dredge from his memory of medical school and practice. There seemed nothing apparent. Bad food or drink remained the most likely culprit, however, so he expected he would be there a couple of days while the patient recovered. Then he would return to London, where he would be a few guineas closer to resuming his research. 'I shall give you a restorative and we shall hope that has you up on your feet soon,' he said with confidence.

'If you say so. You are, after all, the qualified one.'

Simeon smiled at the parson's pleasant manners and drew a bottle from his bag. He poured a measure of the restorative into a tumbler. It was drunk, drawing a slight smacking of lips at the bitter taste. 'I shall oversee the preparation of your meals myself. Perhaps there is something your housekeeper has missed.'

'She has been loyal to me for twenty years, or thereabouts,' the older man said. 'It will not have been deliberate.'

Simeon's brow furrowed. 'No, I am sure it won't.' Momentarily, he wondered why such a possibility should have occurred to Dr Hawes.

'London must be a most exciting city for a young man,' the parson said in an off-hand fashion.

Simeon thought he detected the slightest hint of envy in the divine's voice. 'It's certainly invigorating. Sometimes one wishes for a quiet life, though.'

'Ray and Mersea could not be described as invigorating, I fear,' the older man said. 'But I hope you will stay a few days.'

'Until you are better. Of course.' Another creak from the invisible end of the library made him wonder if there was some pet hiding in the shadows and he glanced again that way but could make nothing out.

'And we have not discussed your fee. Would five guineas a day be sufficient?'

'That would be very generous.' Simeon gazed around at the shelves that enclosed them. 'Tell me, how many books do you have here?'

'Books? Oh, three thousand at a guess.'

'That's a good size for a library. I—' He cut himself off as a louder sound from the gloom made him start. 'What is that sound? Do you own a dog?'

'A dog? Good heavens, no.' Parson Hawes peered up at his relation with mystification on his face. 'You do not know? Oh, I would have thought you would have been informed at the Peldon Rose, if not before.' The Rose was clearly the local hub of social intelligence. 'Well, it is best that you take the lamp and look for yourself.' Slightly suspicious of the roundabout way of informing him, Simeon lifted the oil lamp from the table. It threw a yellow glare around no more than two yards of the floor, illuminating stacks of books and a series of rugs – Persian or Turkish. Fine quality. He went towards the dark end of the room. 'But be careful, my boy,' the older man warned. As he moved, Simeon saw the beam glint again on a reflective surface like the black water of the estuary. Glass. The end of the room was indeed one huge glass panel and the light from the lamp seemed to flit about in its sheen. Then another sound, this time a rustling, emanated from it. He saw his own reflection in the dark pane, like a mirror, coming forward with the lamp in his hand.

As he came closer, the light fell properly on the foot of the glass, rapidly rising up to its full height. And what it revealed seemed strange indeed. The panel was not the end wall of the room, but a transparent partition between the part occupied by Parson Oliver Hawes, with his three thousand volumes, and another smaller section, cut off from the public realm.

'This is rather unusual,' Simeon said.

'It is necessary. Such rage.'

What rage? Simeon wondered, examining the murky pane.

Suddenly, something, a patch of pale colour, appeared behind the glass: a moon-like disc that retreated into the black and disappeared. And something green flashed close to the floor. What had he just seen? Surely it wasn't—? He had an idea, but it seemed insanity itself.

He lifted his lamp to make sure. The beam struggled to penetrate the dark mirror, but he pressed it right to the surface and the light managed to seep through. The scene it lit struck him cold. For sealed behind that glass partition were a writing desk, a table set for dining, a single chair, a chaise longue and shelves lined with books. And motionless on the chaise, wearing a light green dress, sat a woman with dark hair and darker eyes that were silently fixed upon his own.

He watched her, her irises locked to his, her body almost imperceptibly lifting and falling with her breath. Her lips parted, as if about to speak.

'You know of my sister-in-law?' Parson Hawes's voice seemed to come from a long way off. The woman's lips closed again, pulling into a wry, sardonic smile. Then she cocked her head to one side, looking around Simeon to glance at the parson. So this was Florence, who had killed James, the parson's brother, by throwing a decanter so ferociously against his cheek that it broke and an infection set in to pollute his blood. 'We are safe, she cannot get out.' That was clear. This was a cell – a glass-fronted cell bedecked with fine furniture, but a cell just the same. 'Simeon, my boy?' Parson Hawes asked.

The smile remained. It stayed with him.

'I had no idea of this.'

She was, perhaps, ten years older than him, and the curve of her chin and cheek marked her as a rare beauty. In country parts, he thought, where men were sure and direct rather than kowtowing to lineage, she would have been aware of it. She might have used it. And it was a beauty he had seen before, for she was undoubtedly the subject of the portrait hanging above the fireplace in the hall.

'Her presence surprises you.'

'Surprises me! It amazes me,' he stated, returning to himself. 'What is she doing there? How can this be right?'

'It was here or the madhouse,' the parson declared with a note of annoyance, as if angered by an insinuation behind the question. 'After she killed James, the judge was ready to put her away. I have done all I can to keep her safe. But if you think she would be better in a strait-waistcoat at Bedlam, please tell me.'

31

The curate's voice disappeared again as Simeon stared at Florence. She was a striking woman, it was certain. And she was holding his gaze without the slightest concern, as if he was the one imprisoned behind that pane.

'So, she lives in this?'

'She has a bed chamber and washroom behind. You see that doorway.' There was a narrow opening at the rear of her cell. 'So she has privacy if need be. And her food is the same we eat.'

'I see . . .' His mind was racing. No human being should be held like an exhibit at the zoological gardens. And yet she had killed a man, and life in Bedlam would certainly be far, far worse. Simeon had been required as part of his training to enter that terrible asylum: inmates chained to the wall day and night, rocking themselves into madness; others who would scream that they were quite sane, but would have torn at your throat with their teeth given the chance. Very occasionally a patient would be freed, having been cured of their mental affliction, but it was a rarity and only for the mildest patients. No, keep her out of Bedlam if at all possible. Cruel as it seemed, perhaps she really was better off here.

'It has not been easy. It has been a hard balance,' Hawes continued, anger subsiding into something like regret. 'Hard on all of us.' He struggled to wipe his brow with a handkerchief.

Simeon wanted to speak to her, and yet Florence bore no sign of wishing to speak to him. 'How does she get her meals?'

'The hatch at your feet.' Simeon looked down. There

was a rectangular panel in the glass that could be lifted up, large enough to put a tray of food through but little else.

'There must be a way out for her.'

'In order to ensure full security – which is what she needs – there is not. She is quite bricked in. Linen is changed weekly in order to maintain cleanliness, passed through the hatch. Water flows to and from her apartment. Other than that, there is no movement in or out. It has to be thus in order to satisfy the legal authorities.'

Legal authorities be damned, Simeon thought to himself. 'Florence,' he said. And he was sure that her pupils changed at the sound of her name. 'Can you hear me? I am related to you – by marriage. I am Dr Simeon Lee.' He waited for a response, but she remained quite still. The change in her eyes was the only one he would see. 'I am here to treat Dr Hawes for an illness.' And did he then see the slightest alteration in her face? Perhaps the edges of her mouth twitched up a fraction. But the light was low, so he had probably only seen a shift in the lamp's glitter.

'I doubt she will answer you,' Hawes informed him. 'She speaks when she likes, but that is not often.'

Simeon remained fixed on her. 'Will you speak to me, Florence? But a word? A single word.'

'She will not, tonight.'

'How can you know?'

'Because she has had her nightcap too.'

Simeon looked around. 'What do you mean?' He detected something threateningly innocent in those words.

'The doctors who examined her said that she was

suffering from an excess of sugar in the blood. The best way to calm her down was a little laudanum daily and nightly.'

Tincture of laudanum – opium dissolved in brandy – was a common prescription for those of an excited nature. Simeon had indeed seen it used with good effect at calming those whose brains were too hot, but he was not certain that it would have been the ethical course of action in this case. 'She has had a dose tonight?' he asked.

'Her usual amount. The tumbler by her hand.'

For the first time Simeon saw that on a small octagonal table, the twin to the one outside, an empty tumbler lay on its side. And he also saw her look down at it. She was certainly following the conversation. So, her mind was awake even if her body was sluggish. *Of course*, Simeon thought, *that could be the cruellest trick of all to play on her.* Imprisonment behind glass was one thing. Imprisonment in a paralysed body would be a hundred times worse. 'Where do you draw it from?'

The parson indicated a large, lockable secretary cabinet in the corner and produced a key from his pocket. 'The bottle is quite safe, I assure you.'

Simeon tried again to reach her. 'Florence, I'm a doctor. Is there anything I can do to help you?' His hope was not high for a response, but he waited for one nonetheless. It did not come.

'You are a good child, Simeon. Your heart does you credit. But some rivers cannot be crossed.'

He brooded. 'How long has she been in there?'

'Since soon after she killed James. Nearly two years.'

'And she has not been out since?'

'Not for, oh, a little more than a year. For a while she was calmer and it seemed safe, you see. There was a door then, onto the corridor, and I would allow her to sit in here with me of an evening. But then a ... change came over her and I felt it better to have the doorway sealed up.'

Better for you, Simeon thought. *But for her?*

A spark flew up from the lamp so that its reflection rose in the dark mirror. She followed its progress, then returned her gaze to Simeon. He wanted to know the history, how his relations had descended to this strange state of affairs. 'Dr Hawes,' he said.

'Oh, you may as well call me "uncle". I know it is not correct in a strict literal sense, but it will make things easier.'

'Uncle.' He turned to face the parson. 'I know only how she killed your brother. May I know why?'

The divine sat deeper into his sopha, seemingly pressed down by the memory. 'She suspected James of ill behaviour. That is all that I am prepared to say.' The slightest flush of shame appeared on his pale cheeks.

'I understand.' But far from his curiosity being sated by the reply, it was fired.

'I am not convinced that you do,' Hawes admonished him. 'My boy, Ray and Mersea are remote places. More remote than you would understand by looking at a map. Remoteness is bred in spirit.' He shifted his weight. 'Would you be so kind as to pour me a glass of water?' For the first time, Simeon moved away from the woman behind the glass, though he felt her still – perhaps more sharply, even, for not being able to see her. He went to the cabinet where a few bottles stood. The water looked clean enough and he handed a glass of it to the parson. 'Thank you. I was telling you about the spirit of this strange outcrop of humanity. Well, I am forty-two years old. My brother is – was – six years younger. Florence is in between us. Her father is the local squire and magistrate, Mr Watkins. A good gentleman. Due to our ages and the fact that the only other children for miles around were the offspring of fishermen and – well, how should I say?'

'. . . smugglers?' Simeon suggested.

'Let us say, men who are strangers to the excise laws,' Hawes conceded. 'Now, as a man of the cloth, I of course always insist that anything that comes within my house has been properly taxed.' Simeon looked over at the little brandy barrel with the silver ladle ready at its side; he would not have placed money on it being entirely above board. 'And so, we became close. James and Florence were, dare I say it, wilder children than I was.'

'Do tell.' He was still aware that one of the subjects of the conversation was listening intently, albeit in the haze of the poppy.

The parson chuckled at the memories. 'Well, I recall one time I was here happily reading away, Roman history probably, that was my great interest. It still is. They were at Watkins's house on Mersea being tutored in French. The first moment their tutor turned his back, they climbed out the window, ran down to the Hard, cast away their outer clothes and swam through the creeks to the Rose.

They turned up in the middle of the day, soaking wet and wearing only their undergarments. Then they had the gall to hire Morty to row them back again, on the promise of payment from my father.' He laughed gently again. 'Scallywags.'

'They sound it.'

'Oh, but they could be wild. Raging too. When James was, oh, sixteen or thereabouts, they were at the county fair and he was paying all sorts of attention to a farm girl. Florence became quite savage and left the poor girl with a black eye. Well, not very genteel, but they were children. Only children.' A more recent memory seemed to overtake the curate and he stared towards Florence on the darkened side of the room.

'Why does she sit in the dark like that? Does she have no lamp?'

'She has one. Sometimes she lights it. Sometimes she prefers the gloom, I think. It is her choice,' Hawes sighed. 'I am very tired now. I think I shall go to bed, though I doubt I will sleep. I will point you to your room.' He pulled himself up. Simeon tried to help, but he was gently repelled. 'No, I can do this, my boy.' He shuffled towards the door.

Reluctantly, Simeon followed, walking away from the cell that his distant relation occupied. As the light drifted away from it, it returned to shadow; but he felt her watching him still.

'The red door is your chamber. I hope you sleep well,' Hawes said on the landing as he walked painfully away to his own bed.

Simeon bade him goodnight and entered the far bed-room. It was pleasant enough, he found, if a little musty and old-fashioned. *Like the word 'smuggler'*, he thought to himself. He undressed, got into the bed and pulled up the blanket, sorting through all he had heard that evening. He knew he should have been considering what could be causing Parson Hawes's ailment, but he could only think of the woman behind the glass.

Chapter 3

A flock of gulls was cawing when Simeon woke, wheeling noisily about, looking for any pickings on the sea or land. After washing in a basin, he made his way downstairs. As he passed through the entrance hall, he noticed again the portrait above the fireplace and examined it more closely. It was of Florence, he knew now, her head and shoulders under a very bright sky – so bright, it could hardly have been England. No, it had to be somewhere else. She wore a sun-yellow silk dress and had been painted perhaps ten or twelve years earlier – when she had been about Simeon's current age – in front of a most unusual house constructed almost entirely of glass. The artist had demonstrated great talent because there was something almost disturbingly lifelike about it.

Mrs Tabbers was eating cheese and bread in the kitchen, alongside the manservant, Cain, a hardy-looking man with tufts of bright red hair sprouting here and there from his head, nose and ears. Cain was chewing, mashing the same mouthful for so long that Simeon found it astonishing.

'Good morning.'

'Good morning, sir,' Mrs Tabbers replied.

'Is Dr Hawes awake?'

'He is.' It was a little after eight by the clock nailed to the wall.

'I want to make sure he eats well. I'll take him his breakfast, if that's all right.'

Mrs Tabbers seemed amused by the idea. 'You go and serve him fine, sir. He's in the library. Had to help him there myself.' She stacked a tray with bread and milk.

'It is possible that Dr Hawes has eaten something disagreeable.'

'My cooking is very good, sir,' she returned curtly. 'The parson tells me so often.'

'I'm sure that is true.' Not wishing to offend the woman providing him with sustenance, he took a piece of bread to prove it. 'It is possible, though, that something unseen made its way into his meal. Do you eat the same food as he does?'

'Exactly the same. Both of us. No point making it twice, is there?'

'No,' he agreed. 'And the water, milk – all comes from the same source?'

Cain spoke. 'All the same,' he said, in a tone that suggested he thought they were being accused of something and he did not appreciate it.

'Wine?'

'Rare,' Mrs Tabbers told him. 'Christmastide. Communion wine, of course. But that's just a drop and the whole congregation drinks it.'

He was getting nowhere. 'And what about the brandy nightcap he has?'

She shrugged. 'A drop most nights. He finished a barrel a day or two before he fell sick.'

'Which day, precisely, was that?'

'He fell ill on, let me see, Thursday. First of the month.' That concurred with what the parson had said.

'We should test it,' Simeon replied. The timing was interesting. It could conceivably be the source of the priest's sickness, although the continued worsening of his condition suggested it was unlikely. 'I don't know who would want to try it, though.'

'I'll tes' it,' Cain offered.

'What?'

'The brandy. I'll tes' it. Make sure i's safe to drink.'

Mrs Tabbers huffed. 'Fine Quaker you are, drinking. What about that pledge they make you take?' she muttered.

'Quiet, woman,' he snapped. 'Fer medical reasons.'

Simeon interposed. 'You understand it could be a risk.'

'I'll give it ter me dog firs'. Nelson. He likes a drop o'

41

brandy.' There was no accounting for the risks some people would take for drink. Cain checked the clock. 'Do it 'bout nine. Jus' got ter see ter tha' foal first,' he told Mrs Tabbers.

'What foal?' Simeon asked.

Cain shovelled more food into his mouth and spoke as he chewed. 'Lame 'un. Born few weeks ago ou' of parson's mare. See if i's better now. If no' ... well.'

'Well what?'

'A drain, isn' it? Costs good money. No good ter the parson nor me. Don' wan' a lame animal.'

'I see.'

'No' a good sign, lame foal.' He chewed his food slowly.

It occurred to Simeon that country folk put great store by the health of their animals, and there was a lot of augury in how the livestock fared. So yes, an ill foal was a curse. 'Are you from Mersea?'

'Born 'n' bred,' he grunted. 'Never been more'n ten mile away.'

That could be useful. 'So you know all the secrets around these parts,' Simeon said jovially. After seeing Florence the previous night, there were certainly some secrets that intrigued him.

Cain put down his cup. 'Ye have somethin' ye wan' ter ask? Ask it.'

The reaction was more aggressive than he had expected; still, there was no point denying his curiosity. 'What happened between Florence and James?'

Cain cut a hunk of bread, buttered it and ate, seemingly stringing out the action to decide on a form of words. 'They say Mr James was involved in thin's.'

'Peter!' Mrs Tabbers warned him.

'Well, i's the truth.'

'What sort of things?' Simeon asked.

'That's enough gossip,' the housekeeper said firmly.

'Mrs Tabbers . . .'

'No. Enough gossip.' She poured herself a cup of milk from a jug and set it down as a punctuation point to the conversation.

Simeon thought it best to retire from pressing them for now. He would catch more flies with honey than vinegar and so he left the room, taking the tray of the parson's food to the library.

He entered, keeping his line of vision firmly on his patient, to find Hawes on the same seat as the previous evening, a blanket drawn over him.

'Good morning,' the parson mumbled.

As he set the food down, Simeon could hold back no longer and slowly turned his head to gaze at the other end of the room. She was seated, quietly watching, wearing the same green dress. It might have been the only one she was allowed. She could have been there all night. Did she sleep? Simeon would have been unsurprised to discover that that pleasure, that release, was unknown to her.

But he had to tend to his patient, who was in poorer health than the previous night. His skin was pale, and when Simeon measured his pulse rate, he found it faster and lighter, indicating a worsening of whatever condition ailed him.

'My boy,' the curate said, 'I feel as if an army is marching about in my head. An army.'

Simeon carefully lowered his uncle's wrist. 'I'm sorry to hear that. Have a little breakfast, it will be of benefit.' The parson ate and drank some, before beginning to shiver and collapsing back onto the sopha. 'It's true you're a little worse, sir. But I'm confident you will pull through.' He was lying. The man's signs of life were far weaker than before. It would have been no surprise if he had fainted then and there. 'If you could—'

'Someone is poisoning me!' Hawes suddenly cried, arching his body up, then crashing it back down.

It took the doctor a moment to get over his astonishment. 'Why in Heaven's name would you think that?' he asked.

Hawes panted and recovered a little. 'I am not without enemies.'

Another astonishing claim. The man was a country curate, not a Turkish pasha. 'Enemies? Who?' But despite his scepticism, one identity inevitably suggested itself. Simeon looked to the glass box. She was watching, quite unperturbed. 'Do you mean Florence?'

'Her. Others.'

Simeon's overarching doubt returned at the suggestion of a whole cabal of assassins on the island of Ray. 'And they are capable of poisoning you?'

'More than capable. More than capable,' he insisted. 'You must find out what it is they gave me. There has to be a cure.'

It was not unknown for patients to become delirious during fevers, blaming phantoms for their sickness. Most likely, the priest was suffering a perfectly normal organic disease or possibly accidental food poisoning. And yet the vehemence of his claim, the history of homicide at Turnglass House and the subsequent strange incarceration of the parson's sister-in-law gave rise to creeping, amorphous doubts in Simeon's mind.

Whatever the cause, it would be best to keep the patient calm. 'I must say, if you have consumed poison, either accidentally or by someone's deliberate action, it is a strange poison that continues to worsen continuously for six or more days after ingestion. I don't know of any that works that way,' he said. 'And the food and drink that you take has all been consumed by your servants. They have not suffered so much as a stomach complaint.' He went over to the new barrel of brandy. 'You have drunk from this, haven't you?'

'It was new the day before the illness took me. I have not drunk from it since then.'

'That makes it very unlikely to be the source of any harmful compound, though Cain's keen to test it anyway.'

'Oh, let him. Why not?'

At that, Hawes, exhausted by the interview, turned over and fell to dozing. Simeon watched over him for a while and, with little else to occupy him, took the time to meander among the bookshelves. They were a strikingly diverse collection – from the religious to natural history to prose fiction. *The Twelve Caesars* here; a collection of Donne's poetry there.

Tap. Tap. Tap. He looked up. The sound of slow, light clinking of glass against glass. It was coming from

Florence's end of the room, where she was rhythmically tapping a tumbler on the partition between them.

'Florence?' he said. 'Do you want something?' She unfurled a finger to point. Simeon followed its line to the priest's octagonal table. On the surface, suggesting recent usage, was a book. He picked it up to find it was a slim novelette. *The Gold Field*, it was named, in appropriately golden lettering. 'You want to read this?' he asked, holding it towards her. 'You want *me* to read it?' Her hand dropped to her side and she returned to her chair.

Simeon turned its dry pages.

I'm going to tell you a story. It isn't a nice story, it isn't really a nasty one. It's just a story. It's a true one, though, and I can put my hand on my heart and swear to that because I was there.

You've probably never heard of me. You might have heard of my father, though. If you're from California, you probably heard his name every time you went to buy whiskey, let alone glass for your windows. I don't think I'm giving away any family secrets when I say the ban on alcoholic drink was a godsend to his bank account. Before Congress decided we all had to take the Pledge, he was a doing-okay man of business. But a cousin in the city of Vancouver – that's in British Columbia, if you don't know – and a natural disposition to make money by any means necessary meant that through the Twenties the barrels came sailing down the Pacific and Dad swapped them for cash. Lots of cash.

The first thing Dad bought was a new suit. The second was a wife. The third was a house made out of glass.

Not all of it, of course. There were timbers and there were metal frames and wood floors. But the walls were almost all glass. That made it hot in the summer, cold in the winter. My father bought it from a man who had built the place and then lost all his money in a stocks scam that Dad said he really should have spotted as a con. The seller thanked my father for taking it off his hands, as if he was doing the fellow a big favour, though the truth was that my father had seen some carrion lying out on the grassland and swooped down to gobble it up.

And now we begin the story, because it has to begin. It begins in February 1939.

Simeon closed the book, keeping his thumb between the leaves, and examined it more closely. Florence had wanted him to read this, so there had to be some significance he could not yet see. The book was no larger than the average cheap novelette, but was handsomely bound in veined crimson leather. Who was the author? He checked the spine. It carried the name 'O. Tooke'. Whoever he was, he was writing about the future and describing it as the past. He opened the pages again.

The snow had come down the day before. We don't see it very often – no more than every few years out on the coast, where our house was built. Back when most of California had no name, not even an Indian one, somebody called the headland where we live Point Dume, and it suits the name. When I was a kid, the snow would fall on the beach where the sea hit the sand and there would be this crazy up-and-down white layer, like albino skin stretched over a dragon's ribs.

Now, you need to know who was there at the time. The principal characters would include myself, my younger sister, Cordelia, and our grandfather. Then there was my father. My mother had passed away five years earlier in France. I had carried her coffin.

We usually dined late, in the French style, taking supper at nine-thirty. By that time, of course, most of us were on the brink of starvation and the best-fed people in the house were the servants who got to eat three hours before us, their so-called masters.

That evening, I descended the staircase and caught sight of my sister slithering into the dining room wearing a Chinese-style dress that sparkled with gold fibres.

'I can hear your thoughts,' she called over her shoulder as I followed her across the black-and-white tiles.

'What am I thinking?' I returned.

She stopped, waited until I caught up with her, took my arm and whispered in my ear. 'You're thinking that there are just a few more of these dinners to get through before you can get back to Harvard and that nice girl who sends you poetry so bad it should be illegal, but which you keep re-reading because she has a very pretty smile.'

I coughed. Sometimes her insights cut too close to the bone.

It was right then that the butler cleared his throat, his way of getting your attention without actually asking for it.

'Yes?' I said.

'A letter for you, sir.' He handed me one on a zinc platter. It was sealed all around with wax tape and had my name on the front in a handwriting I didn't recognize. It looked like it had been written in a hurry – the ink was smudged and the stamps were stuck on at a crazy angle. There were a number of them, because they were British – this had come all the way from England. And there was something inside the envelope that skidded about when the letter moved.

Not knowing what to expect, I tore it open and pulled out a small card. Its message was short.

'I will tell you what happened to your mother. Charing Cross railway station in London. Beneath the clock. March the seventeenth at ten in the morning.' And left in the envelope was a silver necklace with a small locket. I opened it to find a tiny picture of my mother smiling. I knew it well. She had worn it on the night that her carriage had spun off the highway in a violent storm. No one had known where she had been going that night. Only now someone did. Someone who hadn't signed their name.

So, the story was a quest. A quest for the truth buried in a family history. Not so unlike what Simeon was living right then. Although the words were simple enough and the story was – as yet – unthreatening, still he felt a growing unease with it. As if it were pulling him somewhere else, to another time, to someone else's world. 'Florence? This book. What does it mean to you?' he asked. 'Why do you want me to read it?' She made no reply in words or actions. He turned to a later page. The landscape became strangely familiar.

The pub looked shut, but I smacked my fist on the door loud enough and often enough to raise the dead. And finally, the landlord came out looking like he was one of them. So this was where the smugglers met. Some were inside with pistols in their jackets.

Simeon flicked to the end of the story. It came, unusually, halfway through the book and was followed by blank pages.

So there he was. And there I was. And nothing between us except a hatred that burned like hot coals. I could have put a knife in his ribs and said a prayer of thanks to the Almighty while I did it. For all his declaration of love and piety, he would have done the same to me in the time it took to cuss. The question was: which of us had the plan, and which of us had the gut-ache to put it into practice? In the end, I did.

'Florence, what is this?' he asked.

She looked at the book he held, then rose from her seat and went to her own shelves. She plucked out a thick volume, leafed through it until she found the page she was looking for and took a pen from her desk. She circled some words on the page, then brought the page to the glass. Ringed in black ink, he read: *Warning. Revelation. Premonition.* The last was circled twice. She returned the book to her shelf and reclined on her chaise longue, watching him.

Chapter 4

Simeon did not want to admit it to himself, but he was, in fact, relieved to close the crimson novelette and place it in the tallest bookcase. He noted as he did so that his hand was actually shaking. Only then did he peer through the glass to Florence. She did not seem disappointed or angry at his failure to read every word. She looked satisfied, as if making *The Gold Field*, and its American vistas and ocean-spanning story, part of Simeon's life was enough for now. More would come of it, of that he was certain.

With his patient asleep, there was little for him to do other than hope that Hawes would rally. True, he could take the parson to the hospital in Colchester, but what good would that do? It would only expose him to the dirt and germs with which such provincial hospitals were awash. No, he was better off here, where Simeon could monitor his condition.

'Shall we talk, Florence?' he asked. She settled her face deeper into her palm. 'Is there something I can do or get you to make you more comfortable?' She smiled, but it was to herself, he thought. It said that she pitied the man trying to tempt her to speech that would never come. 'Well, if you ever think of anything, I should be delighted to furnish you with it.' He put his hands in his pockets. 'Will you tell me about yourself?' Nothing. And, on the spur of the moment, something more provocative left his lips. 'Will you tell me about James? Will you tell me what you did and why you did it?' He did not know what reaction to expect, only that he wanted to spark one. 'Did you love him or did you hate him?'

And then it came – no screams, no tears. She only drew herself up to her full height, lifting her face to the unseen sky as if bathing in sunlight, and then sighed, with a whole world of words in that one sigh. Then she left for her private space behind the public, where she would be alone. Was the emotion that she had felt regret? Shame? Longing? Anger? It could be all of these or none.

Just as she disappeared from view, Cain entered the room with a plate of bread, some salted beef and a cup of milk on a tray, which he set on the floor before the glass wall. He lifted the hatch and kicked the tray through. The cup turned over, spilling the milk onto the food. He left the room without a look back.

'Cain!' Simeon yelled after him, outraged.

'You must forgive Cain's rough manners.' Hawes had woken and also witnessed his servant's actions. 'He was most attached to my brother.'

'Does that justify this sort of behaviour?'

'One must try to understand the anger of others.'

Well, there was little to be done. But still there was the brandy to test. Simeon took the small barrel downstairs and called for Cain, who attended with a sullen expression until he saw the keg of drink.

'All right, this is your opportunity,' Simeon said, irritably. He wanted to discipline the servant for his earlier behaviour, but it was not his place. 'But try it on your dog first.'

Cain did not need asking twice. He went outside and returned with an ugly-looking hound.

'This's Nelson,' he muttered. He filled a bowl with a mix of the brandy and water. The dog lapped it up – Simeon wondered if the dog really did like booze, as Cain had claimed. They waited twenty minutes and the dog began to stagger about, then fell flat on his face on the kitchen floor, but remained breathing.

'Good stuff,' Cain said. He poured himself a brimming tumbler of the drink.

'You should wait until tomorrow before you try it; watch Nelson for any change.'

Cain shrugged and put the glass to his lips. Men around here were probably weaned on the stuff. Cain sipped it cautiously at first, smacking his lips ruminatively, then poured it down. 'Good stuff,' he confirmed.

Simeon hoped he would not now have two dying

patients and one expired dog to tend to. 'Just wait here a while, I'll watch you.'

'If ye like.'

He calculated what he would do if Cain showed symptoms of poisoning. A purgative would be best. He had a bottle of water filled with mashed mustard seeds that would cause a man to bring up in seconds whatever he had drunk. But they waited thirty speechless minutes and there was no change in Cain's complexion or pulse rate, and Simeon calculated that that was probably it.

The servant thanked Simeon and left, carrying the remains of the barrel and the paralytic canine.

Simeon wandered outside in Cain's wake. It was a foul morning of near-horizontal pricking rain. Over the sea itself, he could see a haar forming – the freezing sea fog that could envelop entire towns, turning them into pits of cold haze.

He strode across the sea lavender, determined not to let the weather defeat him. Turnglass House occupied the sole solid part of Ray, on the western edge of the islet, surrounded by mud and lying a few hundred yards from the Strood. But it was still exposed to the very worst that the North Sea and its Viking ghosts could hurl. As he stared north-eastwards, across neighbouring Mersea, to those countries that had spawned the wild men and their armed longboats, he could well believe there was something malignant in the landscape, ready to leap up and drag a man to his death.

For a second, as he looked that way, something glinted at him from the mud. A sparkle catching the sun's weak rays just for a flickering moment, then gone again, leaving only the waterlogged ground. He stared where the glimmer had been, but there was nothing now.

The channel that separated Ray from Mersea was in a quandary, surging forward and back, thrusting up towards the Strood, threatening to overwhelm it and then retreating when it found its strength not quite enough at this hour. And someone was making his way along the causeway from Mersea: a boy aged around twelve, carrying a basket on each hip, who was moving quickly, in a practised fashion. Simeon watched him step off the Strood and place one of the baskets on the ground. It held a few packages wrapped in paper and string.

'Are you the butcher's boy?' Simeon called over. The boy nodded a shallow, suspicious nod. 'Don't you bring the meat right to the house?' He jerked his thumb behind him. It was hardly a long way for the lad to venture. The boy shook his head from side to side. 'Why?' The child stood stock still, like a bird watching a cat. 'Tell me.'

The suspicious child hesitated. Then he broke into an evil sort of grin and recited a tuneless schoolyard rhyme. 'Don' run slow. Don' run fas'. Beware the lady in the glass. Whether ye're cat or whether ye're mouse, shun all who live at Turnglass House.' He stayed briefly to savour his courage, then turned tail and ran back to Mersea. Simeon watched him disappear, splashing through the water as it encroached on the path. Mrs Tabbers emerged from the house and collected the basket with a polite nod. This was, it seemed, a normal ritual on the bleak island.

He returned to the house to find Mrs Tabbers preparing

luncheon from the meat the boy had brought. For want of anything to do, Simeon watched her at work until she asked him to stop. He retired, frustrated, to his room, to read a medical journal right into the evening, only emerging to dine or to check on his patient and glance at the glass cell at the end of the room. It remained empty and he wondered why she would not appear.

Simeon woke shivering. At first, his mind was as blank as a cloud and he had no idea where – or who – he was. All he knew was a shooting cramp in his icy limbs. Slowly, shapes evolved through the darkness, picked out by moonlight, and he was able to discern a bed chamber: a taper in a candlestick holder by his bedside and his coat over a chair. He sank back into the pillow, momentarily exhausted by the effort of recollection.

Yet it was not just the cold that had woken him. A rattling from the window told him that it had come unfastened and was clinking in the wind. He rubbed his eyes, feeling a thin layer of ice crystals on them, and forced himself out of the bed. The freezing air woke him fully then, and even after he had secured the window, he was unable to return to sleep so that, as he lay, his senses became attuned to the night and his hearing locked on to a rhythmic wooden creaking like that of a ship at sea. It was too regular to be the weather. It was more like human footsteps.

Immediately, he reached for the candlestick, struck a lucifer match against the mattress and filled the room with an orange glow. An old clock over the mantel showed the time to be after two in the morning. It was too late for the parson to be abroad, too early for Mrs Tabbers to be lighting the fires. The house was lonely but not remote, so thievery was not out of the question. Simeon took the iron poker from the fireplace.

The sound of powerful waves – inaudible during the daytime, when people and animals were stirring – whished through cracks in the walls as he looked out into the corridor. All was still and dark.

All except for a bar of light under the door to the library.

He listened. There was no footstep-creaking now. Whoever it was had stopped still. Perhaps they had heard his movement and were now waiting for him. Cautiously, Simeon padded to the library. He stopped, straining for any sound from within, but could hear nothing. His heart beating hard, he raised the poker above his head, ready to bring it down hard on the skull of any intruder, and stepped inside.

The room he found was a strange inversion of the one he had first entered. Then it had been bright in the main room and dark in the cell at the end. Now it was the translucent prison that held the light, blazing bright from a lamp, and all the rest was gloomy, with fingerish shadows reaching from the furniture and books.

Florence's tread had made the sound, for she was there, wide awake, in her usual dress. But it was only her back that Simeon saw, bent as she was over her little table, scribbling on a sheet of paper just visible in front of her. Her hand was making long strokes across the page, followed by short back-and-forths, as if she were drawing a picture.

Transfixed by the nocturnal sight, he lowered the poker and watched.

Suddenly, her hand stopped dead in its motion. Her body froze and her back began to slowly unfurl like a serpent's. Her hands smoothed down her dress. One fell on the page, drifted across its surface to the edge and lifted it from the table.

She never turned to see him, but she stooped to the hatch through the wall, pushed the paper through and snuffed out her lamp. Immediately, she was in darkness again and the glass was a mirror in which his reflection, lit by his glowing candle, stared back at him. He heard her dress rustle. 'Wait,' he said, wanting to hear her voice. The rustling stopped. He moved forward. It started again, then faded, and he knew she had gone.

He bent to examine the page she had left. She had, indeed, been drawing. The flickering candle showed a house on the edge of a cliff. Bold, sweeping lines. A clifftop house at the edge of a wide plain. But the landscape was not Ray. It was somewhere far distant. The scene in the portrait above the hall fireplace.

Chapter 5

The following morning, Simeon decided that some fresh air might be of benefit to his patient and Hawes consented to be wheeled outside in a Bath chair, swaddled like a baby. The atmosphere was certainly fresh. 'Take me over there, will you, my boy?' the parson asked, pointing to the edge of the mudflats. Cain and Simeon carried the chair over the uneven ground, setting it down where the priest could look out to sea. Waves came and went, birds above circled and dipped down for skittering fish. Simeon fell to calculating again what could possibly be causing the old man's sickness. He needed his medical texts, but, frustratingly, he had left them in London. A thought hit him: the library was stocked with tracts on a wide range of subjects – might he be lucky enough to find something useful to his quest there? He could do with Hagg's work on diseases of the gut, or Schandel's on . . .

His thought was interrupted as he noticed, at the edge of his vision, a small clutch of people gathering on the Strood – seven or eight adults and the butcher's boy he had seen the previous day. Even from where he was, fifty yards away, Simeon could see the nasty smile on the boy's face. The child was speaking and Simeon was sure it was the same schoolyard rhyme as before.

The adults were roughly dressed: fishermen or farm workers and their wives. They were eyeing the three men from the house as if watching beasts in a cage.

'What do they want?' Simeon asked.

It was, unusually, Cain who answered. ''Fraid o' us. Think we're goin' ter eat 'em live.' A short grumbling sound from his throat could have been an approximation of laughter.

'It grieves me to say that Cain is right,' Hawes said. 'My flock have not always been the most welcoming and accommodating. Some of them, I say, have been known to be suspicious to the point of, well—' He broke off.

'Of?' Simeon prompted him.

'I could not rule out violence.'

Simeon bit his lip thoughtfully. He had been dismissive of the idea that his uncle was the victim of deliberate poisoning, but was it time to consider the hypothesis more seriously? 'The sickness from which you suffer. Do you think it could be—'

'I am being poisoned. I have told you. Could it be the

sinister hand of one of these seemingly harmless folk? I would rule it wholly possible.'

There was, indeed, something in the expressions on the faces of the villagers ranged before them that said malefi-cent violence was not unknown in these parts.

'Are there any whom you actively suspect? One with a grudge against you?'

Hawes squinted. 'That one on the end.' He pointed an emaciated finger. 'Charlie White. Only twenty years old and yet I have long detected the presence of the Devil in him. Riotous drinking, a use of women for his own purposes. I have warned him from the very pulpit to end his libidinous ways. It fell on deaf ears. I believe he enjoys coming to each service to hear what is in store for him.'

'Is that so?'

'It is. He quite revels in it. He takes pleasure in his sinful rebelliousness. My revulsion at it, he enjoys all the more. But he will not enjoy the endless torment. No, sir, he will not! And he has not the wits to avoid it.'

'The wits?'

'Oh, it takes a mind to escape the fires. He has none. He will burn.'

Simeon made note of the claim. 'Anyone else you suspect?'

Hawes hesitated, cleared a film of mist from his square spectacles and placed them back on his nose. 'There. Mary Fen.' He indicated a squat little woman with hip-length hair. 'The woman has had five daughters in as many years. None of them survived more than a month. Neglect, you say? Yes, perhaps. Or perhaps something worse. She would not be the first in these parts to give a girl-child a dose of something rather than raise her. And she knows that I am suspicious.' He grunted. 'Those two, they are on trial not just before me, but also before God. But oh, it could be any of them. The Devil is everywhere. He may have taken over one of them or all of them.' The thought seemed to grow in him, anger glowing below his words. 'Yes, yes, one of these overtaken by the Enemy. His hands within theirs, dripping something into me.' His bony finger stabbed towards the onlookers.

Dr Oliver Hawes DD was a country parson, and country parsons tended to have very rigid ideas about the Devil and evil. To men like him, they were not merely abstract concepts but corporeal realities that one could encounter in the nearest rank alleyway. But Simeon kept coming back to his father's cabled words. '*Turnglass house has always had something corrupt and malign about it. Leave it to God and the law.*' He met the gaze of the boy, who was mouthing that schoolyard rhyme over and over.

After luncheon, Simeon set himself to hunting through the library for medical tracts that might be of use. Something on toxicology would be perfect – he might even find a home companion on folk remedies, or a botanical guide that listed poisonous mushrooms and their symptoms, of use. He spent the best part of two hours searching – at first taking books carefully down and replacing them precisely where they had been, then, as frustration grew on him, angrily tossing them aside.

All the while, he watched his uncle struggle to eat. The

parson was drawn up beside the fire, where a small blaze was oozing heat into the room, with a shawl across his knees. His condition had worsened even since the morning. After a long while, Simeon gave up on the collection and threw himself into a wing-backed seat. Florence was in the private rear of her cell. Simeon glanced towards her empty chaise longue. 'Uncle, does Florence draw pictures?'

Hawes's eyebrows rose and he spooned a little milky porridge to his lips. 'Pictures?'

'Landscapes, that sort of thing.'

The elder man dropped his spoon into the pewter bowl. 'She has been known to,' he said with some effort.

'Does she draw them at night?'

'Why would she do it at night?' Hawes paused thoughtfully. 'I afford her ample time during the day for her pastimes. Why at night?'

'I do not know.' Simeon could fathom no more than the curate could.

'Have you ... seen her?'

He did not wish the clergyman to know he had been stalking the house after midnight. It would seem intrusive. 'No. But I found this in the morning.' He took from his pocket the picture from the previous night and placed it on his uncle's knees. At first, there was nothing. No spark of recognition in the old man's face. And then dark clouds seemed to spread. Hawes's lower lip trembled. He took up the page, peered into it as if there was some great Biblical truth to be found within, crushed it in his fist and cast it into the fire. Simeon was astonished at the reaction to a mere ink drawing. 'Why did you do that?' he asked.

'It is foolishness. For fools. And I want to eat in peace,' Hawes spluttered. 'No more of it.'

Simeon gave no credence to the explanation. There had been hot anger there. 'Uncle, if you want me to investigate what is making you sick, you must allow me to do so. That picture obviously means something to you. Please explain what it is.'

The reaction was instantaneous. The old man thudded his skinny hands onto the armrests and, with some terrible effort, managed to launch himself forward out of the chair, tumbling to his knees. Simeon made to help him back up, but with a flash of fury that bared his teeth like a dog's, the parson knocked Simeon's hand away. Then, like a young infant, he began to scurry across the floor on all four limbs, thrusting the furniture or other obstacles from his path. 'This is my house. My house! I shall command as I please!' he spat. A side table crowded with books was overturned, and then he was at the glass wall, banging on it with his fists.

'Come out! Come out!' he screamed. 'I know you can hear me!'

'Uncle!' Simeon shouted, coming forward to pull the old man away.

'*Come out!*' The fists pounded again on the glass.

And at that, with a swish of her green silk dress, Florence emerged from her sleeping area. She seemed amused and curious at the spectacle of Oliver Hawes on his knees, roaring outside the cell he had built. At the sight of her, the parson stopped his shouting and began to sway. Simeon was reminded of a cobra as it hypnotizes its prey before striking. But this serpent was spent and he collapsed, dropping his head hard to the floor. He was unconscious.

Astonished, Simeon checked for abrasions and, finding none, rolled the elder man onto his back, gently slapping his cheeks until he began to gurgle. 'You need rest,' he said, lifting the parson into a winged chair. Out of the corner of his eye, he saw Florence placidly smiling, enjoying the show. He was sure she had secrets in her heart as to why her guardian had crawled, livid, across the floor to bang his fists against her gilded cage. He wanted to know what they were. He was beginning to lose patience.

There were also a few last remnants of the drawing that had set the ground ashiver, he saw. At the edge of the grate, some small, charred remains had escaped the flames. He plucked them away. It was the edge of the landscape she had dreamed up. There was nothing more than he had seen before – less, of course – but that imagined scene picked out in black ink took on a greater importance now. For whatever it was, it had had the power to spark violent outrage in Parson Hawes. But how?

As he held it, some of the char coming off on his fingertips, he heard the curate struggle to speak. 'That ... world,' he whispered. 'I told them it wasn't real. They should live under God!'

How were they doing otherwise? Simeon asked himself.

Chapter 6

Over breakfast the next morning, Mrs Tabbers served mutton sausages and black bread.

'I wish to see something of Mersea,' Simeon informed her, tucking into the fare.

'Won' take ye long,' Cain mumbled through overchewed mouthfuls.

'Can I walk the Strood now?'

'Ye can.'

That was to the good. He could still find no organic cause for the parson's condition in the house, but one thought did occur to him: it was possible that the cause lay elsewhere in Oliver Hawes's life. It was just conceivable that the source was in the other building where he spent most of his hours. Simeon did not want to be away from his patient for too long, but he could spare an hour or two to run over to the church of Sts Peter and Paul on Mersea.

He hoped that when he returned, he would still have a patient to tend to, because when he had risen he had found Hawes moaning on his sopha, with a temperature high enough to boil water. He was worse, far worse, than the previous day. 'My head, it is beating like it will burst,' the priest had mumbled. A line of yellow spittle had hung from his lips until Simeon wiped it away.

So, after finishing his meal, Simeon set out through a drizzle from the clouds. Mersea was the more substantial island by far, he soon found. The village was a mile along the path, nestling on the south coast of the isle. A solid church spire rose up and four or five dozen houses seemed to crowd around its base. They were, for the most part, fishermen's cottages, squat and sturdy – their incumbents no doubt the same.

The church itself was a mediaeval construction in the English Romanesque style. Inside, stone and mortar were uncovered, apart from the occasional regimental colours – troops stationed on the island during the French wars at the beginning of the century, probably. Simeon began to look around, in the faint hope that something would stand out as a possible cause of the parson's sickness.

He checked the nave and the vestry, examined the dry font, the high altar and the locked cabinet that probably held the communion wine. Nothing seemed untoward and he dropped into a pew dejectedly.

'Good morning,' hailed a voice.

It had come from a man entering the nave. Aged around sixty, the man was smartly dressed – far more smartly, indeed, than any of the fishermen would dream of.

'Good morning.' Simeon waited to see if the conversation would be pushed from there.

'I am William Watkins. Magistrate of these parts.' He sat beside Simeon. There was little company to be had in these parts, it appeared, so whatever opportunity presented itself had to be taken. The man had an old-fashioned style of speech that suggested old-fashioned thoughts.

'Simeon Lee. Doctor.'

'Oh, here for Hawes?'

'I am.' He was not the slightest bit surprised that everyone here knew who was well and who was sick.

'Live, will he?'

'We can hope.' He shied away from saying that they could pray – in these remote places, such a saying would probably be taken as an invocation rather than a turn of phrase. His diary was an empty one, but that did not imply that he would rather spend a hunk of it on his knees in the church.

'Hope, yes. Then back to Colchester, is it?'

'London.'

'Oh, London! Gawd. I spent time there as a young blade.' He chuckled to himself. 'I expect you enjoy it too. Yes. Quite the town, London.' He seemed to lose himself in his younger days.

'You're Florence's father.'

'Oh, oh, yes. Florence.' His voice sank. 'How is she? Don't get over there as much as . . . I used to.'

Simeon suspected there was a reason for that. It was not a long trek and there must have been precious little for a Justice of the Peace to busy himself with on Mersea. No, Squire Watkins probably felt rather uncomfortable seeing his daughter in her strange confinement.

'She has appeared quite healthy when I have seen her. Where she is.' Simeon chose not to mention the scorn that bubbled below the daily blanket of laudanum. 'It is not easy for her, you know.'

'No, no. Quite.' Watkins lowered his head and his lips quivered, attempting to form words. Simeon waited. Years with patients had taught him the benefit of waiting for someone who wanted to speak. 'That box,' he said after a while. 'I never wanted it, you know?'

'I'm sure.' Few parents would want their child held like an exhibit. Probably Magistrate Watkins was not a wicked man, only a weak one.

'It was there or the lunatic asylum. The judge said that.'

'Then she is indeed better off where she is.'

'Oh, yes.' He brightened, as if having found a supporter. 'For certain, sir. Would have had her home with me if the judge had allowed it. Wouldn't, though. Worried I would let her loose, I suppose.'

Simeon paused, wondering how accurate it was to state that the arrangement was at the insistence of some unspecified judge. 'Would you have?'

'Would I?' Watkins seemed to be enquiring of himself, not knowing the answer without testing it. 'I cannot honestly say.'

Can't or won't? Simeon thought to himself. 'Dr Hawes

is seriously ill, but the cause is not clear and I am attempting to ascertain it. Have you been unwell yourself? Or anyone you know around here?'

'Unwell? No, not at all. All very healthy.'

Watkins's presence at least offered the prospect of an insight into the strange events that had occurred at Turnglass House over the past couple of years – events that had already left one man dead and one woman imprisoned and might now be connected to the parson's perplexing illness. But it would be better to win a little of the magistrate's trust before probing.

'I would like to see something of the island,' Simeon said. 'To get the feel for it. Where would you suggest I visit?'

'There's not much to it, sir. And I say that as a man who calls this place home.' He was doing his best to buck himself up. 'Oh yes, it's a harsh old place. But come, we can retire to my house for a little … tea,' he said hesitantly. Simeon suspected it was his medical title that made the magistrate wary of offering harder drink.

'Thank you.'

They walked for ten minutes to the only large house in the vicinity. It was in the modern style, with spires and turrets like a German castle. 'Come on up to the roof,' Watkins said. 'Don't mind the rain. We see far worse.' They climbed through the house, which was more comfortably appointed inside than its outward appearance suggested, up through a trapdoor and onto the roof. Once up there, Watkins happily presented a telescope and invited Simeon to look through it. 'Can see the coast of

Holland if you're lucky. Kent if you're unlucky.' He waited for his little joke to land.

Simeon could see nothing but a violent squall at sea. 'I feel such an outsider here, even though my family – or a branch of them – are firmly rooted here,' he said.

'Ah, yes, it can surely be that way. But we are a welcoming people,' Watkins agreed amiably, if rather inaccurately.

'To tell you the truth, I hadn't even met Dr Hawes before I came here. I know nothing about him, really.'

'Oh, not much to tell. Dependable country parson, sir. No more than that.'

'Everyone has a past, sir,' Simeon countered. 'I think you were quite the young blood once!'

This pleased Watkins such that he began to beam. 'Ha! Indeed, I was, sir. Ah yes, good old days they were.'

'But Dr Hawes must have been a studious sort.'

Watkins hemmed a little. 'Well, yes. Of course, he wasn't always a man of the cloth.'

'No?'

'Oh, no, no. Though I expect he was always destined for it – by temperament, you understand?'

'Oh?' Simeon sounded interested, but not too interested.

'His father, Colonel Hawes – now there was a strict man, an unbending man – wanted his first son for the army. Not the Church.'

'Did he? Then why didn't it turn out that way?'

'Oh, it did. For a short while,' Watkins informed him.

'I don't understand.'

Watkins sat on the crenellation edging the roof. 'The

Colonel was set on purchasing a commission for young Oliver – I told him, I did, I said, "Your boy's not for the battlefield, Henry!", but he wanted a soldier for his first son and that was that. In the end, the best he could do was find a regiment in the Indian army that would take him.'

'Well, that seems fine enough.'

'Oh, you think so, do you?' Watkins replied, warming to the subject. '*Cashiered for cowardice.*'

'No!' And it was a genuine surprise. Watkins looked a little pleased with himself. No matter how much he liked to present himself as the genial country squire, he also enjoyed the gossip of the age.

'As I live and breathe. Rifles regiment, I think – sent into battle in the Duar War. As I understand it – and the details are hard to come by, you understand – he had to be dragged out of the wagon, and within days he had abandoned his post. They had to send a party out to find him. Of course, that also meant he lost his commission and couldn't sell it – came home an indebted coward.'

Well then. The Church did indeed seem a better choice of profession. 'And what about James?' The magistrate stiffened, as if experiencing a sudden bout of nerves. Simeon noted it.

'I . . . I . . .' He peered through the telescope in order to avoid Simeon's gaze.

'Mr Watkins?'

Watkins came shyly away from the spy-glass. 'James was . . . well, he was different to Oliver, of course. Very different. Tearaway, his father thought . . .' He trailed off.

There was something very much on the man's mind that was not being vocalized.

'And what are you not telling me?'

The magistrate shuffled his feet like a schoolboy. 'I . . . I do not wish to speak ill of the dead.'

'Mr Watkins. I should like to know.' The suspicion was growing stronger that his patient's condition really was a product of some of the strange dealings on these islands – and therein lay the road to a cure.

In order to avoid his gaze, Watkins went back to his telescope and bent down to peer through it. 'I can see Holland,' he declared. 'Yes, I am certain that is Holland.' Simeon stepped in front of the lens.

'Mr Watkins. I must know. I could enquire elsewhere. It might cause something of a stink.'

Watkins came away from the telescope. 'James was involved in . . . activity that was not legal.'

Cain had hinted at something of the sort. 'Would you tell me which crimes?'

'I apologize, sir. I have said too much. I must . . . get to work.' He went, nervously, to the trapdoor that had admitted them to the roof. 'Would you come this way?'

'You won't answer the question?' Watkins stared at the trapdoor. 'Then I'll ask another.' He did not wait for a refusal. 'What were the precise circumstances of James's death? And I shall not leave without an answer.'

At this, Watkins seemed to deflate of all air. 'James,' he said, shaking his head.

'Go on.'

'Sir, this is a painful subject!'

'I understand, but more could depend on this than either of us knows right now. Dr Hawes has it in his mind that someone is trying to kill him.'

'*What?* Who?' He sounded genuinely astounded.

'That we don't know.'

'It's not Florence!' Watkins exclaimed. 'I know what you think, but she would not murder a man in cold blood. James's death was an accident.'

'In that case, you will have no objection to telling me about it.'

Watkins was flustered and started a sentence three times before he managed to complete it. 'It ... it was ... it was an evening a couple of years ago. Florence and he were heard arguing. Not for the first time. Not at all.' He looked up. 'Well, this argument was about a woman, it seems. Can't tell you who – some strumpet of James's, I expect. Jealous sort, Florence. Passionate. I could never keep her back when her blood was up. Gave up trying before she was even seventeen. She ...'

'The argument,' Simeon prompted him.

'Yes, yes. Well, they shouted at each other, he denied all, from what I've heard, and then she threw a bottle or something at him. She had been drinking, I think.'

'Did she mean to do it?'

'How could I know?'

'Well, was she proud of her action?'

'Proud? I do not think so, sir. Defiant. Yes, she was defiant.'

Simeon could tell Watkins was keeping something from him. 'Mr Watkins, as a doctor, I would be surprised if such an act alone would have a woman consigned to Bedlam. I believe there is much you are not telling me.'

Watkins let his head hang. He was defeated. 'After James died, Florence began acting quite strangely. She admitted she had killed him, but claimed there was some sort of conspiracy against her. Then she ran away to London, where she utterly shamed herself, and if it were not for a police magistrate taking custody of her, then the Lord alone knows what she might have done. I had to request Hawes take a coach there to collect her and bring her home.'

Well, that was a substantial addition to the story. 'Why did you send Dr Hawes in your place?'

'Why? Because I did not wish to see my own daughter dragged back with an escort of policemen.' He placed his palms over his face. 'And yes, yes, it was shame. I was ashamed that she was mine; that I had not raised her better than that.'

Simeon understood. Shame certainly appeared to be eating the man from within. 'What next? A trial? Hold nothing back now.'

Watkins nodded. 'A trial. At the Assizes. She wasn't fit to attend – she was raving half the time, only laudanum calmed her and then she wasn't up to speaking. The prosecutor said she had to be committed. But I knew the judge, Allardyce. Had a word. He agreed that instead of sending her to the asylum, she could be kept here.'

'In that glass cell,' Simeon said. He was yet to be convinced that her extraordinary incarceration – indeed, any incarceration – was necessary.

'Under supervision, sir! Under supervision! I offered my own home, but even Allardyce couldn't agree to that. "With your father's fond heart, you would not be a reliable warder," he said. But then Hawes offered and Allardyce allowed it. So Hawes had her apartment constructed. It was the best outcome we could gain.'

Simeon had much to say to this, but did not say it. It was time to check on his patient, whom he did not want to leave for more than two hours at a stretch. And so, Watkins led him back down through the house and showed him out. 'Do give my regards to Hawes . . . and to Florence,' he added, with some discomfort.

Chapter 7

Simeon tramped through the village and back along the Strood onto Ray, passing the mudflats that sloped into the channel between the two islands.

As he approached Turnglass House, dreary in the rain, the curious hourglass weather vane slowly turning on its peak, he gazed at those expanses of clayish mud that Cain had warned him to stay away from. Insects ruled over them and rivulets of silty water coursed through them. But he had always had a contrarian streak, and Cain warning him to beware simply resulted in his determination to examine them as closely as he could.

He drew to the edge. They were as foul as Dante's descriptions of the Styx. He could well picture the ferryman Morty in the role of Phlegyas, transporting souls across the fifth circle of Hell. He was about to move on when something caught his eye. Something metallic was managing to glint in the dismal weather. It was surely the same thing that had reflected the sun's rays the day before but then disappeared from his vision.

Carefully, he picked his course, testing his footing until he found solid earth. Five yards away, it seemed that the prize was lodged on a short, thin stick, caked with mud and washed up from God knows where. Closer still and the metal solidified into a pewter ring. Stretching, his fingers closed on it and pulled it towards him, but the stick was lodged in the mud. Evidently, there was more below the surface because it would not come away. He shifted his position so he could reach it; then he pulled harder. And without a moment's change, without a warning in the mud or the sky, he found he was not grasping a sliver of wood but the freezing, filth-encrusted forefinger of a man's hand.

He fell back and stared at what he had held. Buried in the mud was a part, or the whole, of a man. It was a vile image even for those such as he, who saw the dead and dying by the week. But he drew himself together. A cadaver was a cadaver whether it was on a slab or submerged in the ground. And someone, somewhere, was waiting for news of their brother, son or father.

Bracing himself more firmly, guessing the weight of what lay in the mud and quelling any latent human horror at the scene, Simeon set out to reveal the hidden dead. He gripped the palm of the corpse-man, as if they were shaking hands as friends, and heaved.

With a little effort, first the fingers, then the wrist lifted into the light. A dripping, mud-spewing shirt cuff emerged, a metonymic caricature of man's vanity. Yes, it seemed the whole of this poor soul was down there.

Simeon took grip of the cloth and pulled, levering against the soft ground upon which he knelt. And yet with all his strength he could not manage it. Neither, though, could he leave to get help, for he knew that the hand might then be covered up once more, and the body could sink so deep, or be washed away in the channel, that it might never be found again. He had no choice but to get closer.

So he slithered chest-first from the solid ground to the watery mass of mud, feeling it ease over his own body and submerge his splayed legs. He knew he was sinking an inch at a time. If he miscalculated, he could end up interred in the same rough grave as the buried man. Carefully, then, he delved deep into the mud, along the solid flesh of the dead man, until he felt shoulders. The rain was coming down heavily now and his back was soaked with it, but he refused to let his charge disappear once more.

He braced himself. And with all of his strength, he heaved. Inch by inch, it started to move. Closer it came, and deeper he slipped, until they were embracing in the dirt. There would be empty eyes, a throat clogged with mud, but Simeon could only think of hauling this cold body into the light.

He squirmed around until, snake-like, with a yell and the last of his strength, he finally writhed his body and its dead burden to the solid ground. He collapsed, panting with the effort. With his palm he wiped mud from his own face and spat out brown water. And then he caught sight of the man's face for the first time.

Caked still in mud, it was barely recognizable as human rather than a primordial being. But there it was: a forehead, thick nose and jutting chin. A heavy-set, muscular man who must have once breathed, worked, eaten, laughed and cursed. Simeon stared at what he had dredged from the mud and let the raindrops wash away some of the dirt.

Who are you, my friend? he thought. *Did you drown? Did your heart seize while you were walking? Have you been missed and searched for or has no one noticed your absence?*

The flesh of the body was almost wholly intact. There was some rotting here and there, but little to see. Either the death had been recent, or the clay had perfectly preserved it, as if it had been set in ice. Simeon pulled back the eyelids. The irises were clear and green; the teeth strong but discoloured by tobacco – one of the local fishermen, perhaps.

He considered what to do. He was only a few hundred yards from Turnglass House. At this point, he might as well haul the body there himself. So, with supreme effort, he heaved the man aloft onto his shoulders and slowly made his way on to the house.

When Mrs Tabbers saw what awaited her on the threshold, her mouth drew into a silent scream. 'Calm yourself,'

Simeon instructed her as she staggered back. 'He is quite dead.' He pushed past and headed for the rear parlour, not concerning himself with what he was tramping through the hallway.

There was a table overflowing with religious texts that he swept to the floor and replaced with his burden, mouth up, dirty water dripping to the carpet.

'What in God's name . . .' the housekeeper whispered, having recovered her voice.

'A man, Mrs Tabbers. A dead man.'

'Who is it?' He noticed her surreptitiously cross herself. No doubt the parson would have a thing or two to say about such papistry.

'You will have a far better idea than I have.' He took a vase of flowers, cast the blooms aside and poured the water over the corpse's face, wiping as he went with the doily upon which the vase had been set. Puffed-out cheeks appeared through the remaining clay.

'John White. Tha's who't is.' Cain had entered, drawn by the commotion, and the words were his.

Simeon was opening the man's collar to examine him. He stopped at the name. 'John White?'

'Aye.'

The previous day, when the locals had ranged before them on the Strood like crows, Hawes had pointed out a young man he suspected of many ill deeds, named Charlie White.

'Is he Charlie White's brother?'

'Was Charlie's cousin. No more. Gone now. Look't 'im.' Cain rubbed his jaw.

'So he was from here? Mersea?' he asked.

'Mersea, aye. Dis'peared a year or two back.'

'Well, I think we now know why.'

'Aye.' Cain stepped forward. Mrs Tabbers kept a greater distance. Whether it was respect for the dead or fear of the dead, Simeon could not say. But as a doctor, he felt little of either. To him, cadavers were primarily evidence of medicine's failures.

'Who was he?'

Mrs Tabbers and Cain exchanged a subtle glance.

'Oysterman.'

'I see. And what else?' He waited a moment. Cain returned Simeon's gaze. 'You're hiding something, aren't you, Cain?'

'Hidin' nothin'.'

Simeon fixed him with a look. 'Keep it to yourself for now, but I'll find it out.' He had deep enough suspicion as it was. It seemed the whole population was in on the local criminal trade.

'You do tha'.'

Simeon returned to the body. A dark pool had formed below it on the rug and he set about stripping away the clothing. 'Bring me scissors, cloths and a bucket of warm soapy water,' he instructed Mrs Tabbers. 'And you'll want some sheets to catch it.'

'Shall I wake Dr Hawes?' she asked.

'No, I'll let him know myself later.'

She hurried away to fetch the water. 'Tell me more about this man,' Simeon instructed Cain.

'John? Quie' sort,' he said in a still-sullen tone. He

clearly thought this was not outsiders' business. 'Strong.' If Cain described a man as 'quiet', it must mean he was virtually dumb.

'How did he go missing?'

'Summer the year before las'. Found his boat overturned and run aground on the Hard. Him no' in it. All though' he'd drowned in the sea. Looks now tha' he drowned in the mud.' He squinted through the window. 'Wouldn' be the firs'.'

'Did he have family?'

'His ma died a few months back. He'd a sister, Annie, but she lef'.'

'So Charlie is the closest?'

'S'pose he is.'

Simeon stripped off his upper clothes. They were soaked with rain and mud. Mrs Tabbers returned with the hot water and sheets and he washed and dried himself, then wiped away more mud from the man on the table.

The skin was yellow all over and frayed in places. But as his jerkin was cut away, the flesh of his torso seemed to explode outwards. Mrs Tabbers let out a shrill scream.

Simeon looked down at the ruptures in the flesh. 'Something has been eating him.' Cain mumbled an oath. 'Mr Watkins should be informed.'

'I'll go,' Cain said.

'Thank you.' A thought occurred. 'But don't tell Charlie White. I shall see to that.'

Cain narrowed his eyes. 'If ye like.'

Simeon cleaned up, climbed the stairs and changed into a fresh shirt. It was time to tell the parson.

Entering the library, he found Hawes lying on the sopha, moaning. A glance to the partition at the end of the room showed it to be empty, its inmate out of sight in her apartment behind.

'Uncle,' Simeon said.

The old man's voice was little more than a whisper. 'Oh, Simeon, my boy. I am caught in such shivers.' Simeon placed his hand on the priest's forehead. He was indeed cold to the touch. 'I am not long for this world.'

For once, a patient might be proved right about the gravity of their condition.

Simeon had lost patients before, of course, but always strangers. He hated the idea of allowing his relative's life to slip away, however, because it was his responsibility. 'Don't write yourself off yet, Uncle. You'll be up and delivering sermons to the flock before you know it.'

The older man managed a thin smile. 'I am not so sure,' he wheezed.

'Is there someone you would like me to fetch?'

Hawes lifted his eyes with an effort. 'No one. There is no one. Your father is my closest blood relation. If I die, this house will go to him, and then, in time, to you, you know.' His eyes opened wide. 'What will you do with it?'

Do with it? Among all the other strange thoughts that Turnglass House had engendered over the past few days, the idea of inheriting the place had not been one. What could he do with it? Instantly, he thought of his research, stalled for lack of coin. If he could somehow convince his father to transfer the house to him immediately – his father had, after all, declared a deep aversion towards the place – he could sell it and restart his work without having to grub around for paid employment or grants. He could devote all his time and effort!

'I'll use it to help discover a cure for cholera, Uncle,' he said. He knew it was a little pompous a statement, but it would give the curate comfort, no doubt, to think of some good coming from his death.

'Oh, that would be a fine use. Yes. But there must be one condition.'

'And what is that?'

'If I die, you must become responsible for her.' Simeon looked sharply to the glass cell at the end of the room. 'It is for her own good. If she is released, she will be immediately caught up and sent to the madhouse.'

Simeon had no desire to become Florence's gaoler. And yet he considered that the parson was correct in his assertion that Bedlam was the other outcome. Well, if it all were to come to pass, he would do his best to treat her fairly. That would probably entail a period of observing her and deciding on the best course of treatment or action. If they were both lucky, her liberty would be achievable. He gave his uncle his word that he would do as asked.

And then the information that Simeon had come up to impart could wait no longer. 'Something has occurred that I must tell you about.'

'Oh?'

'I found the body of a man in the mudflats.'

The parson's head lifted a little in surprise. 'Good Lord, who?'

'I believe his name was John White.'

'John White? Oh, he's a local boy. So that's what happened to him. Poor young man. It happens, you know. Even to those who live here. Poor young man.' He looked to Heaven and whispered a silent prayer. 'Would you like my aid with the arrangements?' he croaked, his consciousness drifting away.

Simeon doubted his uncle would soon be in much of a state to aid with anything. 'I will see to them all. Cain can help.'

White's body would have to be kept at the house until then. He resolved to have Cain remove it to the stable. Mrs Tabbers was unlikely to appreciate having it stretched out on the rear parlour table indefinitely.

With the revelation of the body of John White, Simeon wanted immediately to speak to White's cousin, Charlie, whom the parson had identified as one of Mersea's malefactors. Hawes would likely be out of consciousness for a while, so Simeon took directions to White's home from Cain. After that, he would visit the other person on Mersea that the parson had pointed out as a potential murderer, Mary Fen, who had lost five daughters in infancy. As Hawes had said, she would not have been the first poverty-stricken mother to pour something caustic into her child's drink rather than attempt to feed another mouth. And the baby farms, those places in the stinking cities where women would permanently leave their unwanted children, paying a lump-sum for their upkeep, were notorious for it – the case of Margaret Waters of

Brixton, who had poisoned many infants in her care before being caught and hanged at Surrey County Gaol, was still fresh in the memory.

White lived in a cottage away from the main settlement. It was picturesque in a pastoral style: there was wisteria around the door and the window frames were painted green. And yet Simeon could not put his finger on it, but there was something seedy about the house, as if there were rot in the roots of the wisteria.

White lived here alone, having recently inherited it from a relative, Mrs Tabbers had told him. As soon as White opened the door, Simeon concluded that the well-kept appearance of the cottage was down to the deceased woman and would not last long. White was young and handsome with it. But although each part of his face was fair – the jaw was strong and his complexion clear – still Simeon could not dismiss the impression that, like the house itself, there was something sour about the whole.

'Are you Charlie White?'

'Ye come ter me home. Ye know who I be.' There was a sneer behind each word.

From time to time, in the course of his work, Simeon had had to deal with aggression from some such as White. It did not bother him.

'You are right about that.'

'An' I knows who ye be.'

'I am glad of it. Dr Hawes . . .'

'Dr Hawes,' White sniggered contemptuously.

'Yes. He is ill.'

'Then le' him pray.'

'I'm sure he is doing that. He thinks you might know something of his illness.'

'Thinks wha'?' And he laughed a deep, guttural laugh. 'I know nothin' of wha' ails parson.' He leaned in. 'Bu' I know wha' them tha' lives in tha' house desires.' He stopped laughing. 'Wha' they wan's an' wha' they does ter get 'em.'

There seemed to be meaning beneath the verbal confusion. 'Tell me what you mean.'

White hesitated. 'Ask th' woman. Th' mad one's killed parson's brother. If any knows, she knows, now her hubby be dead 'n' done. Ye people say th' Whites don' deserve a taste o' justice. Well, seems maybe we can sup it up anyways.' He made a slurping sound with his lips and started to close the door. Simeon stayed it hard with his hand.

'Your cousin's body has been found.'

'Me cousin?'

'John. He was missing, wasn't he?'

White narrowed his eyes. 'He were. Where'd they fin' him?'

'In the mudflats. He's at Turnglass House.'

White huffed scornfully. 'Where else would he be?' And he shoved Simeon's hand away and slammed the door closed.

Simeon chewed over White's words. For sure, Turnglass House seemed the centre of all these strange events. Simeon's father's claim that there was something malign about the house was becoming truer by the minute. Well, he would think it over as he made his way to his other house call.

Mary Fen lived in a fairly proportioned little house, Simeon found. She blinked in surprise at Simeon's presence on her threshold before giving him admittance – it must have been rare that she had a visitor, let alone one with clean clothes. Her husband, who was some sort of metals artisan, peered over from his work stand, then returned to his labour without a flicker of interest.

Simeon looked around. The place was reasonably well appointed. A few pieces of simple furniture. A rough rug on bare boards. 'Mrs Fen.' She blinked hard. 'I am Dr Lee. Parson Hawes is my patient. I saw you two days ago on the Strood, watching us outside the house.' He waited for a response. There was none but the hard blinking again. 'Why did you do that?'

'Didn' mean anythin' by i', sir. Hones'.'

'So why do it?'

She mumbled her answer. 'Parson don' like us.'

Simeon watched Fen's husband pour a small amount of powdered metal into a wooden dish and mix it with some other compound. He drew out an amalgam on a small glass spoon. 'Why do you think that is?'

'Don' know,' she answered sheepishly.

Simeon could tell this would be a less forthcoming conversation than the previous one, where Charlie White had enjoyed sneering at the clergyman. 'Did you know Dr Hawes is unwell?'

'Had heard somethin'.'

'What had you heard?'

'Jus' he was a-sick.'

'Do you know how he came sick?'

'No, sir.'

'Do you know anything about the household?'

'Not me, sir.'

He changed subject and asked her what she knew of John White. Blinking harder than ever. She knew him, of course, but they were not friends. What of his cousin, Charlie? She had nothing to do with him. And so on and so on.

'Do the people around here talk of what occurs at the parsonage?' Simeon eventually asked.

'They . . . talks.' Her husband began brushing the amalgam over the handles of a box of steel knives on his table. Simeon was distracted by the man's work.

'And what do they say?'

'They says tha' wha'-was-'er-name . . .'

He guessed who she meant. 'Florence.' There was something about the man's actions at the work bench.

'Tha's 'er. Tha' she killed her husban'.' What was he using on the steel?

'That is of public record. What I want to know is . . . Wait!' Simeon stood up and went over. Fen's husband stared up, amazed at the interruption to his work. 'Those knives.' He pointed to the cutlery. 'You're silver-plating them.' Fen blinked hard, just as his wife did. It seemed to be a family trait. Simeon shook his head. He could barely believe that the root of the family's misfortune was so tragically simple. He placed his hand on the artisan's shoulder. 'You have lost a lot of daughters,' he said softly. The man before him sighed deeply. 'You have been . . . suspected of poisoning them, have you not?' He regretted the pricking of the accusation, but there was no way around it.

91

'Some people—'

'Well, I am sorry. But you *have* been poisoning them.' Simeon lifted one of the untreated steel knives. 'The amalgam you are using.' He tapped the knife on the side of the wooden pot. 'It's silver and mercury, isn't it?'

'Aye.'

'Well, the silver powder is harmless, but the mercury—'

'We made sure the babies never touched it!' Mary insisted.

Simeon softened his voice in sympathy. 'I am sure you did, but mercury is a wild metal. That is why we call it quicksilver. We now know that it can seep into the air and you can breathe it in.' He looked at her. 'I'm sorry to say that you were breathing it in even when pregnant and it would have passed through your blood to your unborn daughters. They would have come out of the womb already poisoned.'

'They were ...' the husband began, but broke off, bewildered.

'I'm sorry, sir. We adults can take that level of poison in the air, but your daughters' chances would have been null,' Simeon said, placing a hand on the man's shoulder and hoping that the knowledge would bring some sort of comfort. The words hung in the air and the couple before him stared at each other, unable to speak. 'If you want to try again for a child, I can advise you how to do it safely.'

Well, the parson's suspicion of Mary Fen seemed unfounded. But Charlie White was surely no stranger to dark intentions.

Back at the house, Simeon found his uncle sitting up, with a letter clutched to his chest and a pen on the floor beside him. He refused to say what the missive contained. 'I'll fetch you a restorative,' Simeon said, after taking the cleric's pulse rate. He went to his room and poured a glass of tonic, although he was not optimistic about its potential to help. Despite the claims of his tutors, he had always been convinced the drink's effect was more on the mental being than the physical.

When he returned with it a few minutes later, the parson's eyes were closed and he was mumbling to himself.

'Drink this, Uncle,' Simeon said, putting the tumbler to the older man's lips.

Instantly, Hawes was awake. He threw the drink aside, shattering the glass.

'Damn it! Someone is poisoning me!' he cried out. 'I am being killed. It must be her!' His arms writhed in the air and Simeon fought to hold them down – the parson's sudden strength was an amazement after his weakness a few minutes earlier. Simeon could think only of the death throes of a tiger.

'She cannot get anywhere close to you,' Simeon insisted. 'She has been trapped behind that glass wall for more than a year. If anyone is poisoning you, then it is someone else.'

'Then find out who!' the parson snarled. 'Find out! I will not go to my maker in this state.' He whispered something that Simeon could not hear. Then he spoke out loud again. 'If I die, do not let her out. The judge said that she must not be allowed out or she will be taken to the madhouse. Promise me you will not. Not until it has been settled with Watkins and the authorities.'

'Uncle—'

'You must swear.'

'Must I?'

'Yes. Just think what will occur if she is let loose in contravention of the conditions prescribed by the judge.'

Simeon disliked being forced into such a vow, but he relented. His uncle was probably correct that the due process should be followed, otherwise he would probably be cut out of the subsequent decision entirely.

'I do swear it.'

'I am glad. Here. See that this is sent.' He shoved the letter into Simeon's grasp. 'You may read it.'

It was addressed to the bishop.

My lord Bishop,

I beg your most profound indulgence in a private matter. I believe I am the subject of an unholy crime. Someone unknown is doing me to death with the use of a foul poison. Poison, my lord. I make no bones about it. I beg you to send such an inquisitor as will discover the identity of the devil. I know for one that the woman of whom I have guardianship harbours fury towards me, due to my position, although I take on the wardship as a duty to keep her from the madhouse. If not she, then one of my servants or one of the local people who have fomented a secret hatred in their hearts towards me. My nephew, Dr Simeon Lee, knows the identity of those with the greatest reasons to wish me ill.

I remain, my lord, the most humble servant of the Church in your figure.

Oliver Hawes DD

'You want me to dispatch this?' Simeon asked, perturbed.

'Yes. And send for the constable. I want people subject to questions. They must give up their foul secrets or face *peine forte et dure.*'

Torture? It was not the fourteenth century. 'I don't believe there are sufficient grounds for such an action.'

'There must be. It must be sent.'

Mrs Tabbers entered the room. 'I heard something break, sir,' she said uncertainly.

Hawes leaned over the side of his bed and vomited. The servant ran to clean it up with a cloth pulled from a pocket in her apron, while the parson recovered, his eyes blazing.

'I understand, Uncle,' Simeon said. He had severe doubts about the instructions, but it was no time to argue. He tried to understand what lay behind the parson's sense of persecution – it was not uncommon for the brains of the dying to take eccentric turns, even paranoid ones. But if someone nearby really was behind Hawes's illness, it was clear that it could not be Florence. She was where she always was.

And yet Simeon had to admit that poison now seemed a plausible explanation after all. If there was an infection, it was nothing he had seen before and nothing anyone who had been in contact with Parson Hawes exhibited signs of bearing. It could be some sort of internal injury or disease, but there would be no way of knowing without cutting the man apart. 'Mrs Tabbers, would you be so good as to spend the night in the house? I think Dr Hawes needs constant watch.'

'Of course, sir.'

'Tyrone!' the parson barked. 'Fetch Tyrone, he will find who is doing this to me.' He tore his square spectacles from his face and threw them aside as if they burned him.

'Who?' Simeon, bemused, asked the housekeeper. He had never heard the name, but a man does not call on his deathbed for a distant acquaintance.

'Don't know, sir,' she replied, concerned only with cleaning.

Simeon bent down to the parson. 'Who is Tyrone? Is he important? Does he know who is . . . poisoning you?'

'He will find out, I say!'

'Then tell me how to find him.' But the cleric only glared, pulled back and squeezed his eyelids closed. His chest sank, as if all the strength had once more evaporated. It had been an astonishing display.

'Would Mrs Hawes know who this man is?' he asked the housekeeper.

'I don't know, sir.'

Simeon approached the cold wall of Florence's cell and stood before it. His fingers stretched of their own volition towards the reflecting glass.

As if she had been waiting for him, she stepped out from her private apartment and met his gaze. Hers seemed somehow deeper and more forceful than it had been. As if she were returning to herself.

'Do you know what the matter is with Dr Hawes?'

She smiled but said nothing. The previous occasions had taught him to expect such a response. But was it hiding knowledge or ignorance? He could not tell.

He tried another tack. 'Who is Tyrone? Dr Hawes wants him here.'

The woman behind the glass laughed lightly to herself, lifting her mouth and stretching out her throat as she did so. He saw the long, aesthetic line of her throat. Then she turned and passed back into her private room, with the light rustle of moving green silk.

Chapter 8

'Please, sir! Come quick!'

Simeon was shaken into sickly consciousness. The housekeeper's face came into view in the light blue that exists only a little after dawn.

'Mrs—'

'Dr Hawes. I think he's dying!'

Simeon staggered from his bed, not bothering to throw clothes over his nightshirt, and grabbed his medical bag.

The library gas lamps on the wall were lit, but low, affording the room a dim yellow wash. One look at his patient told him the man was on the edge of the precipice between life and death.

'Uncle! Dr Hawes!' he shouted. He slapped the man's

grey, unshaven cheeks. 'Wake up!' He lifted the eyelids, looking for a pupil reaction to the light Mrs Tabbers held aloft. There was none. He tried *sal volatile* beneath the man's nose, blowing air into the man's lungs and shaking his chest hard to get the heart beating.

But it made no odds. Because regardless of the actions prescribed by his textbooks, Simeon knew his patient had expired. The colour was already draining from his lips; there was no pulse in the wrist or neck. No, there would be no more sound, no more fury from the curate.

Upon his weary instruction, Mrs Tabbers departed to fetch Cain from his cottage on Mersea, and Simeon dropped heavily into an armchair. A pang of anger shot through him then and he swept all his instruments from the octagonal table. A jumble of tongue depressors, the useless stethoscope, the heavy bottle of restorative that had never restored, all went tumbling to the floor.

So now there were two dead men at the house. Here, a priest who should have been preaching his Sunday sermon that morning; and outside in the stable, John White, cold as the mud whence he had been dragged. Turnglass House had become a morgue.

'Don't be sad, Simeon.'

The voice echoed around the room. It came from everywhere at once. It was low, as if it drifted in the black water and Sargasso weed of the creeks. And every bit as cold. Finally, that voice.

'Florence,' he said, to himself, not to her. He stared at the dark glass. He could see nothing behind it, but she was there, he knew.

And then it surrounded him again. 'He always dreamed of being plucked up to Heaven. And now ...'

There was a spark in the black as she lit her oil lamp. The glow filled her room, casting her grainy shadow to the floor. He stood and went to her. He could see his reflection twice – once in the glass and once in her irises.

'I thought you would never speak.'

'And then I did.' Her voice had a defiant hint of the local accent below the fine tones of a squire's daughter. It was tugging weeds below the smooth surface.

He glanced at the corpse on the sopha. 'Now that he's dead.'

There was a long pause, heavy air. 'Yes. Now that he's dead, I have found my voice.'

'Do you know what killed him?'

She cocked her head to one side, amused. 'You're the doctor.' She was enjoying the game of evasion.

'Do you have an idea?'

'In here, Simeon?' She waved her hand. 'How could I have any ideas at all in here?'

He wondered if that were true. 'So why are you speaking now?'

She sat and stared into the oil flame. 'I think it's that I want to. I want to hear myself.'

'I want to help you, Florence.'

'You came to help Oliver, Simeon. That didn't turn out so well.' She smirked a little.

'My medical training only goes so far.'

'Oh, I know that. It took two doctors to put me behind this screen.' She leaned forward and tapped the lamp

100

against the glass. 'Such learned men. All that training it took to know that I was best placed here so as not to endanger myself, or them or any other men.'

He wondered where Mrs Tabbers was, how far away Cain lived and how long it would take for them to return.

'They did their best, I'm sure. What people are capable of – that's something we can't learn in a lecture theatre.'

She glanced at the dead priest. 'Oh yes, that's certainly true. People are astonishing at times. The things that I have done, what the others who lived on this godforsaken place have done. I would never have predicted them. No.'

His brow furrowed; there was so much she was holding back. 'What are you talking about? Florence, if you know something, tell me.' She made no reaction. 'Who is Tyrone?' he asked. 'Dr Hawes wanted him here.'

'I'm sure he did.'

'So you know him?'

'You could say that we have met.'

'Can you tell me where to find him? Dr Hawes said he would know who was poisoning him.' The information would be too late for a doctor and medicine, but in time for a judge and the rope.

Florence sat back on her deep blue chaise longue. 'I don't want to meet him again. If you knew what he had done to me, you wouldn't either.'

That gave him pause, but still he had to press on. 'Do you know where he is?'

'Yes.'

'Then for God's sake, tell me where.'

Instead of answering him, she began to sing to herself, a sweet, sad hymn. '*Abide with me; fast falls the eventide. The darkness deepens; Lord, with me abide. When other helpers fail and comforts flee, help of the helpless, oh, abide with me.*'

It did not help him; it seemed a mockery. What would convince her? 'Dr Hawes was good to you. He kept you out of Bedlam.'

'Have you considered that that is where I belong?'

The words were a surprise, but he had no doubt that she meant them. And it went some way to explaining why she had not immediately demanded her liberty after Hawes's death. 'You have no idea what you are saying.'

'How so?'

'I've been in that foul pit. You can't imagine what goes on there.' The game she was playing was beginning to irritate him.

'Enlighten me.'

'Enlighten you?' His emotion widened into anger. 'In the Devil's name, I'll enlighten you. I've seen men take their own lives by drinking the vitriol used to clean the floors. Would you like to know how their screams sounded?' He did not wait for an answer. 'I've seen women give birth and offer their own children up if the men overseeing them would only let them out. My God, I would rather beg on the streets than consign someone there. So no, I will not see you, nor any other human being, degraded to that.'

He strode around the room and ended standing over Hawes's body. Simeon had lost his patient, but that made him doubly determined to find the cause of the man's death. He thought back to his lectures and recalled one old professor ordering the eager young students to 'consider the environment' when looking for cause. Was there something in the surroundings that he had missed? Hawes had been so certain that he was being poisoned. What if he was, but not by human hand? Toxins could slip so easily into the home – arsenic in the wallpaper, for instance, or mercury in knife handles.

He tore the room apart.

To laughter from the glass box, he upended the chairs, pulled books from the shelves and threw the rugs aside.

'What is it that you are looking for?' she taunted him.

'Whatever killed your brother-in-law.'

'I doubt you'll find it under the Indian rug.'

Half an hour later, he rubbed his aching back. Nothing. Was the house keeping something secret from him? Or was Hawes himself? His eye fell on the locked secretary cabinet.

The parson had shown him the little iron key that he kept in his pocket. Well, he would guard it no longer. Extracted from the dead man's waist, it twisted in the cabinet's lock. The front panel turned down to reveal numerous drawers inside, and within them Simeon found the usual assortment of writing implements, ink, *et cetera*. It was an attractive piece of furniture: decorative brass-work on the cabinet was wrought into images of birds, fruit, weapons; while a horizontal panel supporting the stack of drawers was decorated with a painted relief of a crowned man asleep below a shining North Star, his name emblazoned below: 'Arthur'. But the cabinet-maker's skill counted for naught as Simeon's hope of a revelation foundered.

He returned to searching the room for anything toxic, all the while watched by the woman behind the glass. He examined again the wallpaper, the leather on the chairs, the rug, but there was nothing out of the very ordinary.

And then his gaze fell on the secretary cabinet again. There was something about that painted panel that itched in his mind. King Arthur slumbering. It was a legend that every schoolboy knew: Arthur was not dead, but sleeping upon Avalon: an island hidden from men's sight.

He got up from the parson's seat and checked the cabinet panel, rapping on it with his knuckles. *Yes,* the sound was hollow! So there was a cavity behind. And a cavity in a secretaire could only mean a hidden compartment.

The thought was not matched to a find, however, as the best part of an hour spent looking for a mechanism to open that panel proved to him that the task was more easily considered than accomplished. He was just about to search in the stable block for a hatchet with which to hack the wood apart when he ran his fingers back over the decorative brasswork. It could hide a button. He pressed and pulled, until by chance he pushed two of the little icons at once.

A click and the panel flipped down.

A voice crawled up his back. 'Well done, Simeon.'

The curate had had a secret indeed, it seemed. For

inside the cavity Simeon found something that struck him with astonishment. It was a smoking implement made up of a long, straight ivory-and-terracotta pipe plugged into a square terracotta bowl. Oh, he had seen pipes like this before and knew what they meant. This one was quite remarkable, however – the ivory was delicately carved with intertwined flowers, making an ugly thing an object of extraordinary delicacy.

'Oh yes, well done, Simeon.'

'Thank you, Florence.' He said it with the same irony that had dripped from her words.

'I think that deserves a reward.'

He looked up from the pipe. 'What do you mean?'

'Something that might, in a sense, go with the item that you have just found.'

'Go on.'

She lay along her chaise longue and pointed at the tallest bookcase. 'That book that you began to read.'

He remembered the strange red novelette with gilded letters, *The Gold Field* written by 'O. Tooke', about a man crossing the Atlantic in 1939 in search of his mother. The novelette that Florence had described, without speaking, only by holding up a page with words upon it circled in ink, as a *premonition*. Simeon had been happy to return its queer time-jumping story to the shelf where she was now pointing.

'What about it?'

'You left it too early.'

'What do you mean?' He took it down and flicked to a point halfway through.

There weren't any sailings for New York for a week. I sat in waterfront bars hoping that a stray ship would turn up out of the blue, offering a quick crossing. I drummed my fingers on the table day in, day out, scanning the horizon and every morning sending to the harbourmaster's office to ask if there had been any stroke of luck. There wasn't, of course. So I had to join the scheduled *Floating City*. It was a huge ship, with cabins for more than a thousand people to skim across the waves on its giant zinc skis.

I had less desire to socialize with my fellow passengers than a murderer desires to socialize with the ghosts of his victims. I kept to my berth as much as I could, venturing out for meals and for an hour's walking up and down the deck so that my muscles wouldn't atrophy. I did this after sunset to minimize the chance I would have to speak to anyone. I needn't have worried – the intense scowl that populated my face scared everyone off. I couldn't wait to get on that airtrain to fly to California and confront the devil.

'No, further in,' Florence insisted.

He went to the end of the story, which finished at the middle of the book and was followed by blank pages.

So there he was. And there I was. And nothing between us except a hatred that burned like hot coals. I could have put a knife in his ribs and said a prayer of thanks to the Almighty while I did it. For all his declaration of love and piety, he would have done the same to me in the

time it took to cuss. The question was: which of us had
the plan, and which of us had the gut-ache to put it into
practice? In the end, I did.

'It's empty from here.'

'Is it? Turn it over.' She motioned for him to do so.

He flipped the book in his hands. The rear cover was
plain red leather. But when he opened it, he found the title
page, handwritten in blue ink and fine penmanship, of a
very different book.

The Journal of Oliver Hawes DD.

'Why didn't you tell me about this until now?' he
demanded angrily. 'It could have been important for inves-
tigating his sickness.'

'Perhaps that is why.'

He did not like her insinuation. 'But why on earth did
he write it in the back of this book?' he asked.

'Because that is the very best place to hide it.' And he
knew she was right. Had she not pointed it out, he would
never in a century have stumbled across it.

'His journal,' Simeon muttered to himself.

'He would read it to me at night. To keep me entertained.' She sneered at the words as if they carried a
bad odour. 'He had been reading it to me that day you
found it. And now that it is time for you to read it, I shall
leave you to it.' She retreated into her unseen private
apartment.

He leafed through the cleric's words. Most were trivial

records of days passed in prayer or the administration of parochial affairs. But a few stood out.

16 April 1879

I received a monograph today that was most interesting. It came from the Anglican Communion Corresponding Society and described the old practice of 'sin eating'. The custom was once widespread in the eastern parts of England, and survives in pockets. The generalized pattern is that upon the funeral of a person of standing, a penniless man or woman is given money to attend. Small cakes are baked and placed on the body of the deceased and said cakes are then taken up by the sin-eater and consumed. Doing so, they take upon themselves the sins of the dead man and will answer for them upon Judgement Day in the place of the other. Such sin-eaters are thus shunned like lepers by their neighbours, for they carry as much wickedness in their bodies as the Enemy. They have pawned their eternal souls for their living bodies. A poor bargain.

19 April 1879

James worries me greatly. He has been gambling again. He goes to London, stays at some disreputable club — or worse — and fritters away the money that Father left him. He refuses to tell me how much he has lost — I am sure he is losing, rather than winning; after all, who ever beats the gaming table? — but it must be substantial. This afternoon I found him burning a letter in the grate. There was a crest at the top and I suspect it was from the Westminster bank, with whom he holds his account. I shall pray for him.

3 May 1879

I am quite frantic. It is three o'clock in the morning and James came home half an hour ago. His trousers were wet through even though it is a dry night and they smelled of the sea. He must have been wading in the surf. Why does a man wade in the surf at night around here? There is only one reason.

I confronted him.

'Don't worry about me, big brother,' he said in that infantile tone he adopts at such times.

'I worry greatly for you. For your mortal body and your immortal soul,' I replied.

'Ah well. As for the immortal, you have to understand one thing.' I was terrified, I shall admit. I had a premonition, knowing what he was going to say. I had hoped he would never actually say the words, that he would at least keep them to himself. 'Your Heaven, your G—d. It's all nonsense, man. Don't you see? We live, we die, that's it. That's the whole deal! Dead as a doornail.'

I always suspected, really, that James was an atheist. But to hear the words uttered stopped me cold. Of course, the Lord always knew what was in his heart, so it is no more a sin now than before, and yet the arrogance of it!

'And what of the mortal, then!' I snapped. 'If you care nothing for G—d's law, what about the Queen's?'

'What, old Watkins and his revenue men? They couldn't find their own legs.'

'And what if they do find you?' I insisted. 'What if they catch you with your wares or whatever you call them?'

'Consignments. We call them consignments if you would know. Well, if they do happen to trip across us — not that they would,

we're very careful of times and places — but if they do, then I have this.' He opened his jacket and tucked into his belt was a loaded pistol. I demanded then and there that he take it out of the house. 'Why? Afraid I might use it on you?'

'Do not joke about murder,' I warned him. I was angry, and that itself is a deadly sin, but I believe I was quite justified.

Well, he smirked at me and went his way up to his chamber. And I wish I could say that was the last I heard of him that night. But as I sit to write this journal, the sounds I hear from his apartment are too loud to ignore. The creaking, the laughing. The sounds of fornication. I cannot but hear her too.

5 May 1879

I had barely sat down to begin today's entry when James stumbled in half-drunk. I had only a moment to close this book and turn it right-side up, so that it presented the strange futuristic fable. I managed it, but James spied my furtive movement and snatched it from my hands. 'Oho, brother, what have we here?' he chuckled. And to my consternation, he sat and began to read the story. All the while, I worried that he would turn it over and discover my journal — not that there is anything of which I should be ashamed, but a man likes his private thoughts to remain private, and that is why I keep them discreetly here. After all, I know that even if I were to record them in a normal fashion and lock them away, James would get his hands on the key somehow and pry. No, this intelligent method of privacy keeps them far safer than any lock. And the fact that James read the whole of The Gold Field in the space of a three-hour sitting, not once noticing that these thoughts were recorded in the rearmost pages of the book, has proved to me the efficacy of my method. After reading to the end of the story, he had sobered a little. 'Do you think we will ever be able to fly through the air like that?' he asked, talking about the aerial machines mentioned in the book.

'If G—d wills it,' I told him.

'Oh yes, always "if G—d wills it."' I did not appreciate his mocking tone. 'And what do you think about the story itself – revenge, really, isn't it?'

'"Vengeance is mine, sayeth the Lord,"' I quoted. 'That means it is not for us poor sinners to contemplate.'

'Surely, we have a right to grab recompense from anyone who's hurt us. Just as the hero does here.' He waved the book. As if The Gold Field were as great an authority as Deuteronomy. 'He went through Hell to find the truth about his mother. He deserves his vengeance. It is his for the taking, that's what I understand from this. And isn't the point of reading to make us think about these things?'

'This story is a divertissement. I set store by the message of a more holy book.'

He rolled his eyes in the most infuriating fashion. 'Why on earth do you even bother reading anything except the Bible? Your mind's already made up.'

At that, I asked him to leave. But it did set me thinking: yes, the author of this strange little work certainly seems of the opinion that vengeance is the right of those who have been wronged. I wonder what flex is available in the Bible's words regarding ownership of revenge – for instance: can a man be the instrument of G—d in exacting the due revenge? I do wonder if the author of this red volume – 'O. Tooke' – had a kernel of a grand idea, hidden among his descriptions of hot California landscapes and houses made of glass. I shall have to consider the question more deeply.

The earlier events of this morning, those I was going to record, pale in significance such that I shall not trouble myself now to write them.

9 May 1879

I had a pleasant day on diocesan business in Colchester. The bishop required some advice on administrative matters and I was pleased to give it to him. I dined alone and returned around eight o'clock.

10 May 1879

I was in church today, composing a sermon on greed. I hoped to strike James's conscience with it. Even if he is an atheist, and damned for it, he may still have some moral sense. I was writing it, as I prefer to do, in the pulpit, so I can understand how the words will fly out, when I noticed a fellow sitting at the back of the nave. He was not praying, just sitting quietly. I thought nothing of it, until close to an hour later I looked up and he was still there. I wrestled more with the argument of the sermon, and sometime after, when I put the final words down, this man was still in the pew, having been there nearly two hours without moving.

I went down and addressed him. After all, it is unusual enough to see a stranger on Mersea, let alone one who sits in the church for two hours without a word of prayer.

'I am Dr Hawes, parson of this parish.'

'I have heard of you, Parson,' he replied in a rough sort of a voice.

'What have you heard?'

'Oh, very good things. Very good things indeed. You are quite the inspiration.'

'Oh, hardly!' I said. It was flattering, but pride comes before a fall and I have always tried to avoid such pomp.

'No, no!' he insisted. 'I have heard far and wide of your devotion. That's why I came here.'

'May I know your name, sir?'

'My name?'

'Indeed, sir.'

'It is Tyrone.'

'Oh, like the county in Ireland?'

'Just the same.'

'I visited there as a child.'

'Did you?'

'My father was in the government service after he quit the army. He took us there for three years. Overseeing the collection of taxes. I very much enjoyed my time there.'

We talked more, about Mr Tyrone – though I cannot recall what he said – and about my ministry for the Lord. He approved of all I was doing.

'Well, Parson,' he said eventually, 'I must go home.'

'Where is that?'

'Colchester.'

'You came all the way to meet me?' I asked, a little surprised – and, I must admit before our Lord, not unpleased.

'I did.' He stood up and collected his hat. 'And it has been worth the journey.'

12 May 1879

I overheard James and Florence whispering today. I managed to catch the occasional phrase and it struck me that they were discussing The Gold Field. I thought it most odd, but dismissed the point. I accompanied Mrs Tabbers to the market in Colchester to buy some household wares. They are robbers there, that is for certain. The cost of linen for the bedrooms is quite ruinous now.

14 May 1879

At James's suggestion, Florence has been painting most curiously. She has been composing images inspired by the very volume within which I surreptitiously write.

One of the canvases has inexplicably appeared above the fireplace in the hall. I nearly fell over when I saw it hanging there in place of the bucolic hunting scene that has hung since our father's time. 'What in the Devil's name has happened?' I exclaimed, forgetting myself. Florence, who turned out to have been watching me enter the house after a brief turn around Ray to take some air, burst into what I can only describe as maniacal laughter. 'I never thought to hear you utter that phrase, brother-in-law. Do you like it?' she enquired, standing atop the stairway. I felt colour rise in my cheeks and could do nothing but stare at it further. It was a painting of her – unquestionably, it was her – but set against a scene that was clearly recognizable from The Gold Field. For her person was set before a large house almost wholly constructed of glass and perched upon a clifftop. The sun shone hard, as it does in California, where the climate is closer to that of the Indies than our own. And the

114

clothes she wore were utterly revealing of her silhouette in a way that none but her maid would normally encounter. I was quite astonished.

'I neither like nor dislike it,' I said, for I did not want to appear churlish. It was something that had meant a deal to her, I supposed, and I wanted to make her happy.

Simeon read those words and thoughtfully closed the journal. He descended the stairs and stared at the painting. The California light was indeed reflecting off glass walls, making the whole imaginary house shine like a lantern. He stood for a while, losing track of the tick of the clock. That landscape seemed somehow more real than the one outside the door. He felt in his muscles that he could step forward through the frame and onto that clifftop, into a search for a lost woman.

When his reverie cleared, he returned to the library and sat down once more with the journal. There were more trivial entries, then another not-so-trivial.

17 May 1879

I could bear it no more this night. Sitting, waiting to see what trouble James was bringing upon our house. I remained in my room until gone midnight without a candle burning so he would think me asleep. Then I heard him come to my door and stop outside. I held my breath. The floorboards creaked away and I heard him going out of the house.

First, I crept up to his chamber, to watch over Florence and ensure she was sleeping well. She was. After a few minutes, I hurried out of the house myself. James had a lamp so I could follow him easily.

We made it all the way along the Strood, right to the Hard. He went down onto it and waited. I hid behind a tree to keep spy. There was a ship out at anchor and, while I watched James, seven or eight more men came. They came right by me and

And then, without warning, total darkness fell. Simeon could no longer see the book nor his hand that held it in place. The gas lamps on the walls had cut out.

His medical books had once detailed the quirk of nature that means when one human sense is shut off, others can make up for it. And just so, without sight, his hearing became acute. He could hear his own heartbeat – quicker than natural, heavier too, sending more rich blood through his muscles in order to flee or fight.

His heart was not all he could hear, though.

'What's happening, Simeon?' Florence asked calmly through the dark.

'The gas has cut out, that's all.' Of course, that would not be all, he told himself. If it were an actual leak into the house, they would be in grave danger of poisoning or an explosion that could blow the building apart in its entirety. He stood and felt his way to where he thought the doorway was. But he tripped on something wooden, fell and cracked his head on a table. It pounded as he squatted, waiting for the pain to leave him. Then there was a new sound: the library door opening. And footsteps. Someone was coming in.

'Cain?' Simeon called. 'Mrs Tabbers?' Whoever was

116

in the room, instead of answering, suddenly opened the shutters on a lamp, shining it in Simeon's face and blinding him. 'Is the gas gone?' he asked. But they remained dumb. Instead, the beam swept the room and hit upon the lectern. Simeon, shading his vision, was becoming annoyed by the lack of reply. 'I said, is the gas gone?'

And at that, the light shut off and the room was in perfect darkness again. Whoever was holding the lamp began making their way through the room. Simeon pushed himself unsteadily to his feet.

'Cain, will you say something?'

All he heard in return was a shuffling sound moving around the room. Then the lantern beam blazed again right into him from inches away, making him stumble back as his eyes were seared with pain. He grabbed out at whoever the lamp-bearer was, sure now that they were no friend, but his hands only caught at air. The intruder scurried out of the room, to the stairs.

'I'll find you!' Simeon shouted, scrambling after them. He saw another brief flash of light as whoever he was pursuing found the front door and dashed out. But that left Simeon thrashing about in the pitch black again. Whoever it was, they had obviously turned off the gas and Simeon had no idea where the main tap was. The best he could do was feel his way down the stairs to the hallway, where he knew there was an oil lamp on the table. He found it in the dark, set it aglow and charged outside.

All he saw was the mean, lonely Strood and the gulls overhead. He circled the house and peered into the stable block but found nothing there either.

Back in the hallway, he searched until he found the tap for the gas lamps, turned it back on and lit them. 'Who was it, Simeon?' Florence asked as soon as he set foot inside the library.

'I couldn't tell.' He rubbed the top of his head. He would have a lump there the size of a potato soon.

'Do you know what they wanted?'

Simeon walked over to the sopha. He had a good idea. And the obvious absence of Oliver Hawes's journal confirmed it.

'Yes, I do. I just don't know why. Not yet.' He lowered himself onto the seat. 'Strange little community you have here. Thieves who steal books. Men who shut women in glass. Parsons who die of nothing. I can't think why anyone would live anywhere else.'

'Ray, Mersea – we're different to you people.'

'I'm beginning to come around to that conclusion.' He stood up, winced again at the sheet of pain that wrapped around his skull and headed out of the room.

'Where are you going now?'

'Now? To bed.'

'You're just going to let that man run around?'

'First, we don't know it was a man, and second, yes, I am.'

But as he stood, he noticed something on the floor. The debris of his search had partly hidden it. It was a sheet of notepaper underneath the lectern. He picked it up.

On blue letter paper, headed with the stamp *Metropolitan Police Magistrate, Bow Street, London*, there was a letter to Oliver Hawes. It could only have come from between the leaves of the parson's journal and fallen out when the book was stolen.

December the fourteenth, 1879

Dear Dr Hawes,

It is now some six months since I entrusted the person of your sister-in-law into the joint care of Mr Watkins and yourself. Since I do not have an address for Mr Watkins, I would be most grateful if you could pass this communication to him. For our records, I would like to know the current state of affairs regarding this woman. Has she stood criminal trial, or has she, as you suggested at the time, been confined to a mental asylum? (And what of the other one she was with, Annie White?)

I thank you for your time in this matter.

Sir Nigel Gant KBE, JP

Annie White? It rang a bell. Cain had said dead John had a sister, Annie, who had left Mersea some time ago. What in Heaven's name was this all about?

'Nigel Gant. Police Magistrate,' he said, facing Florence.

Her lips trembled but she quickly regained her composure. 'I don't know the name.'

Simeon watched her. It was almost like seeing symptoms in a patient: a detached series of colourations and movements. 'I don't believe you.'

She said no more.

*

That night again he woke from a dream. He had dragged John White's corpse from the mud only for its eyes to flick open and its mouth to make sounds that became words. Accusations. Confessions. Condemnations. Whom he was accusing, whom he condemned, Simeon could not tell, for the sounds were in the tongue of Babel: every language and none. Only one utterance made sense, appearing and disappearing through the mire of sounds. *Florence.*

Simeon threw back the covers and pulled himself out of the bed. He had to return to the library.

He padded on bare feet to what had once been the parson's inner sanctum. Like last time he had visited in the night, a light was glowing from that room. And just like last time, she was sitting with her back to him. But this time, she spoke before he did.

'Good evening, Simeon.'

'Good evening, Florence.'

'Neither of us sleeps tonight.' She curled around to face him.

'You have been drawing again,' he said, seeing a page and pencils on the table. She inclined her head to one side. 'What have you drawn?'

'Another house in another time.'

The strange palace of glass perched above an ocean, the one from *The Gold Field.* 'Why do you always draw that place?'

'Why do you have bad dreams?'

He paused. 'I would like to know how you are aware that I do.'

'Why else would you rise in the middle of the night? To

see me when no one else is here? When no one else can disturb us?'

'You are suggesting something, Florence.'

'What should I suggest, Simeon?'

Chapter 9

After breakfast, Simeon wrote to his father, offering to make the arrangements for his uncle's funeral and the disposal of the parson's estate. Watkins, alerted by Cain of the sad news, came to discuss it all.

'One thing to consider,' Simeon said, 'is the situation regarding your daughter.'

'You must not let her out!' Watkins insisted. 'Sir, not yet. Not until the law is clear.'

'The law . . .'

'Aye, sir. If Allardyce gets wind that she is loose, my agreement with him is nullified. She will be bound and taken to the madhouse.'

It was as Simeon had promised the parson, but he had

vaguely hoped Watkins would countermand the promise made. Well, she had been behind the glass for two years; it would only be a matter of weeks, Simeon hoped, before her position could be changed. He was unhappy with the situation, but they could wait that long.

'If you insist. We must also speak about John White,' Simeon told him.

'No doubt we must.'

They went out to the stable where the dead man lay on a pair of crates, awaiting the undertaker's visit. Simeon had performed a fuller examination of the body that morning and the corpse had afterwards been cleaned and wrapped in a winding sheet but had started to smell. 'There's something strange,' he said.

'What do you mean?'

'Well, for a start, John was a local boy. To lose his way and end up drowning in the Ray channel seems a little unlikely.'

'Oh, it happens, sir,' Watkins insisted. 'It happens.'

'I'm sure it does, and for that reason I let it pass as a terrible accident. But then there was something else. Here.' Simeon peeled back the winding sheet and pointed to the dead man's midriff. Watkins looked disturbed by the torn flesh. 'I must insist you look carefully through this tear.'

'My God, must I?'

'I'm afraid so.' He took a pen from a tin in his pocket, pulled apart the edges of a hole in the flesh on top of White's stomach and pointed inside. Watkins, looking unwell, peered where Simeon was pointing. 'His ribs. Look at them. What do you see?'

'Why, his ribs, what else?'

'But what state are they in?'

'In faith, sir, how can I say?'

'You see here and here.' There were a series of sharp little notches cut into the lower edge of two of the bones that he tapped with the nib of the pen. The tip of a third rib was missing entirely, lost somewhere inside the torso or the mud. 'These cuts.'

'Stones in the mud, surely.'

'Not a chance. If he had fallen hard on a rock, that could conceivably break the ribs, but not leave these thin marks. They were made by a knife. A strong blade thrusting in three or four times at least.'

The magistrate stared at him, astonished. 'You are certain?'

'I'm a doctor in the City of London. I see knife wounds each and every week. Mr Watkins, was John White involved in smuggling?' Watkins retreated dumbly and sat heavily on a drinking trough.

Well, that confirmed it. Not only was Watkins's son-in-law involved in contrabanding, but so was the dead man in the stall. The connection was there to be drawn.

'I expect so,' the magistrate mumbled after a pregnant pause. 'They all are.'

'I thank you for your time.' He let Watkins go and took himself to the kitchen, where he found Mrs Tabbers and Cain eating a truckle of sheep's cheese. The marshes around would be sheep and goat land; cows would not thrive there. 'I need to ask you something,' he said. Cain stiffened, as if he could hear a difficult question coming. 'There are smugglers in these parts.'

'Are there now?' Cain replied gruffly.

'Where do they work? When?'

'Nothing to do with us, Doctor,' Mrs Tabbers told him nervously.

'I'm sure that's true. Nevertheless, Mrs Tabbers, I need to know.'

'Then find some'un as knows,' Cain muttered.

He felt irritation building. 'Don't waste my time.' There was a long pause, the air heavy. 'John White was involved, wasn't he?'

Mrs Tabbers busied herself clearing away the cheese and plates. Cain's jaw moved from side to side. 'Say he was. Wha' of it?'

'The man's dead, Cain.'

'Drowned. Happens on the mud.'

'I'll bet it doesn't happen to men who were born on this land. Would you be in danger? I don't think so.'

'Don' get your meanin'.' He stared up defiantly.

'I think you do. And just to make it clearer, White was stabbed. That's what killed him. Not the mud, not the water. A knife.' They looked at the blade in Cain's hand, which he was using to cut the cheese. 'I'm not in the mood for absurd claims that his death was an accident. The man was killed and he was a contrabander. So where do I find them?'

'All righ',' Cain grumbled. 'I'm no Queen's Evidence, so no names. But there migh' be somethin' tonigh'.'

'When?'

He grumbled again. 'Past midnigh' fer the tide. Four bells.' He glared up. 'Tha's two in the mornin' t'ye.'

125

'On the Hard?'

'Where else?'

Two in the morning; well, he had stayed awake longer when working nights at the hospital.

He left them and headed to the library. When he entered, the room's prisoner was staring up at the line of windows that she could not reach. He wondered what thoughts travelled through her. She had little to do but let them loose.

There was something new on her table today, something she must have taken from her private room. It was a small, perfect model of the house, but made entirely from glass, like the one in the book, the one in the painting. Like the real house, the rooms on the upper floor had coloured doors: green, blue, red. And behind each of them stood a human figurine the size of a chessman. The tiny statues were waiting patiently for the game to begin; for the gambit to be played and the king to be captured.

'Do you have someone in London, Simeon?' she asked, apropos of nothing.

'Someone?' He understood her aim, but did not want to acknowledge it yet. He wanted to let her play for now.

'Oh, you know what I mean.' She changed her expression to one he had not seen on her face before. It became coy, like a sixteen-year-old at her first ball. She approached the partition, opened her mouth wide and breathed on the cold glass, her breath turning to mist on the surface. Then she licked her finger and carved a crude heart in the watery film. It lived for a few seconds before melting away.

He chose to be truthful with her. But not open. He did not want her to slip inside him.

'No,' he said.

'Have you ever?'

'Yes.'

'Tell me about it.'

'I choose not to.'

'Are you ashamed?'

'Not at all, but you don't need to know. There's no good in you knowing.'

She smirked. 'So you interrogate me for my past, and yet yours is a mystery.'

'I came to tell you that I was going to observe the Hard tonight. Cain tells me there's contraband coming in.'

'Oh. You are still thinking about John White and his part in our story.'

'I am.'

'Then good luck, my brave one.' She touched her fingers to her heart and began to sing that hymn again. '*Help of the helpless, oh, abide with me.*' And he realized why she sang it over and over: he could just make out the tune itself on the wind. It had to be coming from the bells of the church on Mersea. It was such a mournful hymn, a song of resignation.

'Florence, my uncle Oliver is dead. And regardless of the fact that you cannot have killed him, still you will be blamed. You are a woman said to be so mad that she must be kept in this glass cage. They will condemn you to a lunatic asylum at best, and the rope at worst. Do you not see that?'

127

'I see that,' she conceded.

'And yet you don't help me uncover the truth. In God's name, why?'

Her face clouded in thought. 'Because I choose not to, Simeon. It is my life to lose.'

'And you will lose it! Bedlam or the Tyburn tree: either way, you lose it!'

'Then so be it.'

Nobody in this house knew as much as her about what had happened, of that he was certain. How could he loosen her lips? He set to thinking. He had failed through cajoling or via threats regarding her future. But he might bargain with her. Yes, a deal. He needed something to trade. But what?

Chapter 10

A little after midnight, Simeon buttoned his black coat to the neckline and pulled on navy blue trousers. He did not risk a lantern. Tonight, he had to be unseen, but it was raining and there was no sign of it letting up so his chances were good.

He left the only house on Ray and made his way to the Strood. The tide was rising, threatening to reclaim that thin causeway, the sole route on and off the island. Simeon had been on Ray for a week and it was not nearly enough to understand the patterns of watery encroachment or retreat that cut these islands off.

The ground was marshy as he picked his way along, once or twice sinking up to his knees as he missed the more solid turf. It took him an hour to walk a distance that would have taken a quarter of that in daylight. But he eventually made it across to Mersea, passing the silhouetted hulk of the church.

All the while, he tried to puzzle out the events of the previous days and the shifting place that Florence held in them. And he kept coming back to that novelette, *The Gold Field*. Why had it become an obsession with her and James? Why did she produce paintings and models of Turnglass House's American twin made of glass?

The rain was whipping across the island now, soaking his clothes. He gave up trying to wipe the rivulets from his face and just let them stream down. It was hard weather but he barely felt it, fixed as he was on a far greater danger.

Criminals came in many forms and he had no idea if these men were cast from the timid or the brutish mould. But with the murdered corpse of John White laid out in the stable, he would make no rash moves. Whoever had done for White could well have been the man – or woman – who had broken into the house, turned off the gas lamps and stolen the parson's journal. If so, that malefactor was desperate and felt no aversion to murder.

The Hard was a strip of shingly beach. At low tide you would be able to walk out for half a mile on the sand and mud, but now the waves were lapping at the shoreline. It was a bleak, hopeless landscape and a couple of timber sea walls extending down into the waves were the only shelter from the wind. He crouched behind one, wrapping his arms around himself for warmth. He only hoped that he would not be there all night for nothing.

By the time an hour had passed, he had lost all feeling in his feet. He remained in his place, though, determined to see the night through. After another hour he had to shake himself to keep the blood flowing.

But finally, close to three o'clock in the morning, he began to see shapes on the low horizon: patches of black moving towards him at speed. And he heard them too: snorting, the distant whisper of horses. But no thumps upon the ground – their hooves must have been muffled with rags. He crouched lower behind the rotting timbers of the sea wall, hoping the horses and their riders would keep to the other side.

Within seconds, they were on the shoreline. Five of them, swinging down from their saddles. One whistled sharply, and from another direction – along the beachline on the same side of the wall as Simeon – came the sound of trotting. Simeon pressed himself to the stony ground and saw a line of five or six ponies, heavy with packs, led by a sixth man. At their rear, two more ponies were pulling a cart.

The rain-sprayed moonlight was not quite enough to pick out the faces of the men, only glimpses here and there, but one seemed to be in charge, and he was the first to speak.

'All righ', lads. Ge' on.' The voice was familiar, though Simeon was unable to place it. They began unstrapping the packs from the ponies and lining them up on the beach. One of the men lit a torch wound with an oil-soaked rag and held it aloft. Simeon presumed a boat was coming in for the goods. He was very soon proved right.

A large dinghy emerged out of the darkness, bearing towards the shore. None of the men made a sound as it approached. The pack ponies were on the beach path, twenty-odd yards behind the men watching the sea. It would probably take a minute to land, Simeon guessed, and his curiosity was pricked. Very carefully, he eased himself up and stalked across the shingle. The men still had their backs to him and he took the chance to open up one of the pony packs. Wool. No doubt bound for France or Holland untaxed. And the return trade would be spirits and tobacco.

He crept back to his hiding place and watched the men's leader, who had his back to the torch. Simeon needed to know who this man was, for he could be the key to the violent death of John White. And then the moment came as the man turned to his fellows and his face was lit full by the flame. Simeon was taken aback to see it was a man he knew. For the face of Morty, the ferryman who had spoken to him at the Peldon Rose when he had first arrived, was revealed, fired red as the Devil's.

So this was the man running the ring that had included John White and James Hawes. He had to know something about their deaths, then. And surprising as it was, it was a welcome revelation, because the man was gruff – and Simeon would still keep his wits about him – but Morty did not seem the type to wield a knife and bury a man in the mud.

He watched as Morty directed the unloading and loading – all done quickly and with barely a sound. Then the boat was on the water once more and the gang were readying their horses.

'See y'all back a' the Rose,' Morty growled. He took charge of the slow pack ponies himself, leading them on foot along the beach path as the others hied away. It was Simeon's chance, and as the others disappeared into the night, he padded after the ringleader. They had gone a few hundred paces when the ferryman left off leading the ponies and went to the shoreline, unbuttoned his trousers and began to relieve himself.

Simeon took the opportunity to quietly approach the train and check the saddle packs. They were now stuffed full of bottles of spirits as he had expected. He took one out and unstoppered it: brandy. He felt guilty as he deliberately dropped it to the shingle ground to smash.

Morty whirled around, his fingers frozen in the act of buttoning up his trousers. 'Wha'?' he spluttered.

'Are you armed?' Simeon asked.

'No.' The man sounded utterly bemused.

'You really shouldn't have told me that.' He took another bottle and tossed it onto the shingle, where it broke in two.

'Stop tha'!' The ferryman started for Simeon, but hesitated. He was on his own, aged in his sixties and not a big man.

'No need to worry, Morty,' Simeon said. 'I'm not the police, not the revenue men.'

'Then who the hell're ye?' The weak moonlight could scarcely penetrate the drizzle, let alone show a man's face well.

'You met me last week. I'm the doctor here to treat the parson.'

'Doctor?'

Simeon approached him, just enough for the moon-light to show them each other's faces. But he kept more than an arm's length away, just in case. 'I'm not interested in evasion of excise. I don't care about what's in those packs.'

'So wha' d'ye wan'?'

'I found something. Buried in the mudflats on Ray.'

'Wha' d'ye mean?'

'I found the body of John White.'

That brought on a change. Morty's head bowed. 'How did he look?' he asked.

No point in lying. 'Not good.'

'Aye, well. Mud'll do tha'.'

And now to play the only good card Simeon had. 'It wasn't the mud that killed him.'

'Wasn' the . . . ?'

'He didn't drown in the mud or in the channel. He was stabbed.'

There was a pause filled by the wind, rain and waves. Morty's voice fell into a growl. 'How d'ye know?'

'I saw the wounds. Someone wanted to kill John and they went about it the right way.'

'Who?'

'I don't know. But I want to. If you help me, we can find the man responsible. Do you have any idea?' Simeon asked.

'Idea? Oh aye, I've an idea, all righ',' he spat. He came close enough now for Simeon to see him grimace at the thought.

'Then who?'

'Am I t'tell ye?' His voice was contemptuous.

'Unless you would rather tell Mr Watkins.'

Morty considered. Then he spoke, the syllables stringing out for a mile. 'James Hawes.'

It was not an allegation that took Simeon wholly by surprise. For sure, there was bad blood somewhere on this island. 'Why do you think that?' he asked.

Morty grunted. 'Few days 'fore he wen' missin', John says tha' James were from a fam'ly o' betrayers.'

'Betrayers? He was selling you out?'

'Don' know exac'ly wha' he mean'. Bu' from tha' momen', I kep' a watch on James Hawes.'

'And?'

Morty shrugged. 'Never saw nothin' wrong.' *That might only mean he was a subtle man, as well as an untrustworthy one*, Simeon thought to himself. 'Then John dis'pears. So I tells James he isn' wan'ed no more in the business. Tells him to keep 'way.'

That would not have proved popular with James. 'What exactly did John say?'

Morty hesitated, then seemingly decided the truth was in his favour. 'We were in the Rose. Storin' a shipmen' just come in. I says to John tha' James is on his way t'help. John, he cusses and spi's on the groun'. I asks him wha's the game. He says Hawes folk ain' the kin' we wan' in the business. Bu' John won' say no more, no ma'er how I presses him. Now tha' kinda talk give me heebies. I think t' myself exac'ly wha' ye're thinkin', Doctor. Tha' James is blabbin' to Mr Wa'kins. Or worse. Or mebbe he's plannin' on shootin' us all in the back an' takin' over the business. Clever man, James. I don' trus' a clever man. Don' trus' 'em.'

A clever man. And a violent one too? But had James Hawes truly betrayed his partners and murdered John White? The supposition was based solely on the word of a dead man. And even if it were true, it only answered for the death of one of the corpses currently in repose at Turnglass House.

Chapter 11

When the undertaker arrived in a hearse the next day, he respectfully placed the bodies of John White and Oliver Hawes in coffins and carried them – and Simeon – away.

'A slight change of plan,' Simeon said, when they were on their way. The other man looked at him blankly. 'Will you please drive us to Colchester Royal Hospital?'

The undertaker protested but eventually agreed to the change in destination, and a few hours later the two bodies were on porcelain slabs, around which shallow gutters ran to drain the blood and other foul fluids that are released when a cadaver is dissected.

Simeon's hand held the scalpel. Behind him was one of the hospital's thick-bearded senior doctors, a Mr Bristol, who was to supervise the post-mortem examination. Simeon had not objected because it would, in fact, be useful to have a second opinion.

The knife went into the flesh of the first corpse, that of his father's cousin, with ease. It always took Simeon aback just how fragile the human body could be when the right tool was wielded. The hair-thin blade slipped through the dermis and epidermis as easily as if he were cutting into butter.

Death, for Simeon, was a part of life, and one just as fascinating as the stage that came before it. He cut, drew and lifted; but a thorough examination of Parson Hawes's viscera found them to be the normal, complex organs of a man in his forties. No twisted gut, no spots on the kidneys, nothing untoward that would explain his symptoms, let alone his subsequent death. A puckered scar in his shoulder was noted in passing, but it was too historic to be of relevance.

Simeon turned his attention to the contents of the man's stomach. Hawes had been convinced he was the victim of continued poisoning, and while Simeon could hardly check for every compound, there were some that he could rule out. He collected a mass of part-digested vegetables and soupy liquid from within the parson, which he dissolved in a beaker of hydrochloric acid before inserting a strip of copper into the fetid solution, and waited.

'What will it show?' Bristol asked.

'A silver coating means mercury; a dark film would indicate arsenic or possibly antimony – though that would be rather exotic a toxin to find in rural Essex.' He withdrew the strip and examined it in the light. 'And in fact, it is entirely clear.'

'Is that the result you hoped for?'

'It is *a* result.'

He produced from his bag a small sealed jar of red-brown liquid. 'Brandy that I took from this patient's study,' he explained. 'I don't think there's anything in it, but it's worth checking.' It gave the same negative result.

'There are many other toxins,' Bristol cautioned him.

'Of course. But the patient's pupils were not dilated to suggest atropine. If it were a cyanide compound, he would have been dead in seconds, not days. No strychnine convulsions. Something extracted from plants?' he mused. 'It's possible, but whoever dosed him would have gone to a lot of trouble when they could have just bought arsenic from any chemist and said they had a rat problem. But yes, we should be thorough.'

So, for hours, they tested for a plethora of other toxic compounds, finding nothing untoward. Tired, they agreed that if there were a poison in the man's body, it was an obscure one. 'Well, let's look at the other man,' Simeon suggested.

They turned their attention to John White. Simeon cut him apart in the same way. Folding back the skin and muscle exposed the ribs – a dirty yellow, due to their time in the dirt. He examined the damage to the bones through a magnification lens. 'You see these diagonal cuts into the lower three *costae*,' Simeon said.

'I do,' Bristol confirmed.

'You see how they're deeper at the bottom and peter

away towards the top. The weapon was thrust upwards and forwards. Whoever was holding it was behind this man.'

'Coward.'

'Quite.' He lifted away the skin of the neck. 'Yes, thought so. Look, the neck's been broken at C3.' He pointed to one of the higher bones.

'I see.'

'Our assailant probably grabbed him from behind, reaching around the neck, fracturing it, and stabbed three or four times up into the ribcage with the blade. Must have been quite a substantial one, I would say – the bones look strong enough and he's snapped the end off this one.' They pulled away more flesh to look at the lungs. They had been well preserved in the mud and the left lung had clearly been pierced by the knife that had come through the ribs. 'That's the cause of death there.'

'For sure. How was this man discovered?'

'Submerged in a mudflat. I expect the tides shift the mud banks; if they hadn't uncovered him, he might never have been found at all. This wasn't some drunken brawl that got out of hand – whoever killed him meant to kill him, had the right tool and used it efficiently. We're looking for someone who either planned to kill John that night, or habitually carries a knife and is ready and able to use it.'

'A bad business,' Bristol said, smoothing down his beard.

On the way back to Ray, Simeon considered again. Florence was surely the repository of vital information. How to persuade her to speak? He needed something to trade. And then the mental picture that he held of her, always in that household twilight, suggested the fee.

As soon as he entered the house, he glanced at her self-portrait that hung above the fireplace, then went quickly up the stairs. There were the three coloured leather-clad doors he had seen on his first approach: to his bedroom, to the parson's and to the library; and the plain doors to the other bedrooms. But there had to be another. He swept along the wall. And here it was, a little, discreet, narrow opening embedded in the elm panelling, a tiny keyhole indicating how to release it.

'Mrs Tabbers!' he yelled excitedly down the stairs. She came up, huffing and puffing.

'Whatever's happened now?'

'This must be the way to the attic, yes?'

'The attic? Yes, sir.'

'I would like to go up.'

'Why?' She sounded not so much suspicious, as bemused.

'A whim of mine.'

She huffed again and drew a bunch of keys from her apron pocket. A slim iron one fitted the lock and turned. She stood back as Simeon rushed in and up a thin winding staircase into the eaves of the roof.

It was full of boxes, dust and bird droppings. Starlings were roosting in one corner and they cawed, startled, at the sight of him.

'Yes, yes,' he replied to them. 'I won't be long.' He started pulling open boxes and lifting trunk lids. They were full of the ephemera of life: broken household items, discarded linen. And then he found one full of bright colour. He closed the lid and hefted it down the stairs, into the library.

'John White was murdered,' he said as he entered, dragging the case.

'Perhaps,' Florence replied. She was sitting on her chaise longue, waiting for him.

He discounted her evasion. 'Who by?'

She gazed up at the window. 'I wish I could have a window in here. It's not just the light, you see. It's the air. The air I breathe comes to me already tainted, it has passed in and out of your lungs, and the lungs of Mrs Tabbers or Cain. I would like air from the sky, fresh and pure.'

'I can't do anything about that.'

'No.' She sounded sad. 'But one day.' She reached for a pencil that sat beside a sheet of paper on her table. With her fingertip on its lead, she smudged it across the page a few times and admired her work. Satisfied, she went to the small hatch at the bottom of the glass and pushed it through.

Simeon recognized the scene immediately. It was the glass house in California, the one about which Florence and James had developed the strangely keen interest that had angered the parson. Unlike in Florence's self-portrait, the mansion was this time caught in a snowstorm that swirled and smothered. The lines were thin and grey or black, and yet they still had an unidentifiable nature to them that suggested Simeon could reach right through the paper to another world that was peopled with men and women; where a man was searching for the truth about his mother's fate.

The image faded and he returned to the here and now. Florence had powdered her face and her lips were more rubied than the previous day. 'I was thinking about what I found hidden in Oliver's secretaire. That pipe,' he said. He had been struck by the unusual ivory-and-terracotta item. 'It's an opium pipe. I've had to deal with the effects and they're not attractive. It was something that Dr Hawes wanted to keep away from public sight.'

'Oh yes. You would do well to know where that comes from.' She was taunting him with her knowledge.

'Will you enlighten me?'

'Why would I?'

The sheer nihilism of the question struck him hard.

'Because in return for telling me more, I will make you a gift.'

Her eyebrows lifted. 'But I have everything that I need right here. Didn't Oliver tell you?' There was an undercurrent of malice in her voice.

'I am sure there is more that you want.' He lifted the lid of the trunk. The sheen of sun-yellow silk reflected off the glass of the wall that kept him from her. 'You have lived for a year or more in what you wear now,' he said.

He lifted the yellow dress, the one she wore in the portrait in the hall. It was warm in his hands. Below was another one, peach, and then one in crimson.

The edges of her mouth rose. 'Would you like me to dress for you, Simeon?' She gazed at the gift and sat on her chaise longue. 'Well, my brave one. We shall make a bargain. I shall gain clothing and you shall gain information.' She paused thoughtfully. 'You should return to London.

Call at Limehouse. A house on the riverfront with a red lantern. I don't know the actual address, but you can find it, I'm sure.'

He folded the dress and slipped it through the hatch in the glass. She took hold of the sun-blown silk just a second before he let go, and the tips of their fingers touched before she pulled away.

Chapter 12

His breakfast was a rich mutton pie that Mrs Tabbers had taken from the oven with a clatter. She had intended it for luncheon, she said, but since the doctor was going to London for the day, he might as well eat it now. He thanked her profusely.

After mopping up the last of the thick gravy with a hunk of bread, he donned his travelling coat and set out for the capital. He had just stepped out into the fresh air when, without warning, something seemed to shake the very bricks of the house. A rocketing explosion that came from nowhere, before echoing three or four times off the side of the building. Bewildered, his stomach clenched and he whirled around. 'Mrs Tabbers!' he shouted. 'Cain!'

Cain appeared in the stable doorway. In his arm was a double-barrelled shotgun. 'Wha'?' he demanded.

Simeon ran over. 'What was that?'

A sly grin broke over the man's face, exposing five brown teeth and black gaps between them. 'Tha'? Come an' look.' With a certain trepidation, keeping a close watch on the gun, which still had one barrel to discharge, Simeon followed him into the stable. 'There ye go.' There were two narrow straw-carpeted stalls. One – the one where John White had lain – was empty, but in the other the carcass of a young foal lay on the floor, half its head missing. 'Lame fro' birth. Best thin' for 'im,' Cain informed him. 'No use fer lame animals.'

The grin with which he said it made it clear that Cain was taunting the city man.

'Be careful with that gun,' Simeon muttered, leaving the gory scene behind him and stomping towards the Strood.

He made quick time to the Rose, where he hired a trap to take him to Colchester railway station. There he caught the fast train to London, and by the middle of the afternoon he was at Bow Street Magistrates' Court.

'I wish to see the police magistrate, Mr Gant,' he told the porter, who was engaged in sorting mail into low piles.

'His Worship's not sitting today.'

'May I ask when he will next sit?'

The porter consulted a list. 'Monday.'

That was five days away and longer than Simeon was prepared to wait. Gant was the man who had written to Oliver Hawes about Florence and John White's sister,

Annie, suggesting he had placed Florence in Hawes's care following some legal contretemps in London. 'It is a matter of great importance. May I know his address?'

'His address! Lord, do you think we hand out the magistrates' addresses? And have all the desperate beasts from these courts go calling on 'em in the middle of the night? No, sir, I cannot hand over his address any more than I can hand over the keys to the Bank of England.'

It was hardly a surprising reply. Gant would have been in *Who's Who*, with a club listed where Simeon could write to him, but it would likely be no faster than waiting until Monday. Instead, he noticed a signboard affixed to the wall. It pointed to the various courts and offices, and that suggested a different approach.

As the porter turned his attention back to sorting the mail, Simeon surreptitiously followed one of the directions on the signboard, drifting towards a set of stairs leading down into the depths of the building.

Records departments were always below ground, he had found over the years. It could have been something about the temperature being better for preserving paper, but it was more likely that the sort of person who worked in a records department was not the sort to complain about a lack of sunlight. Most of them probably welcomed it.

It was cold as he descended, and damp so that condensation was pooling at the bottom of cream-painted brick walls. He passed a pair of open storerooms containing mops and buckets, a cloakroom for gentlemen and one for ladies, and, at the end of it all, a mottled glass door. 'Files' had been painted cheaply in white on the door. The lock, he noticed, was a modern spring-lock, the type that made sure the door could not be left unsecured by accident. At waist height, there was a separate handle. It was ajar and he stepped through.

He had had a wild hope that the room might be empty, allowing him free rein, but among a labyrinth of stuffed shelves an immensely fat man was trundling a cart and inserting manila folders bound with white ribbon into their rightful places. He stopped what he was doing and blinked in surprise.

'I was looking for Mr Godfrey,' Simeon told him.

'Who?'

'You're not him?' The man shook his head. 'I'm sorry, who are you?' Out of sight of the fat man, he placed his hand over the lock, gently twisted the knob to draw back the bolt, and pressed the latch into place to hold it there.

'Harrison.'

'Sorry,' Simeon replied, and retreated from the room.

He made his way out of the building and up Long Acre, where he found a post office. He then sent a deliberately garbled telegram to Mr Harrison at Bow Street Magistrates' Court, telling him that there had been an accident at his home and he was needed urgently. He sauntered back to the court, waited half an hour for the telegram boy to scurry in, another minute for the clerk to rush out, and went down to the files room where the latched spring-lock allowed him entry. He stepped in and released the latch so that it locked behind him.

The clerk probably lived in the suburbs – Stockwell or

Clapham, perhaps – which would give Simeon a good hour-and-a-half to rifle the files and discover how and why Florence and Annie White had been entrusted into the care of Parson Hawes by a police magistrate. But if Harrison lived closer, he would not be so lucky with the time. He set to work.

The files were arranged according to the district where the crime had taken place and the date it had occurred. But even presuming a crime *had* taken place – involving Florence, Annie or both – Simeon had little idea where it could have been. His best pointer regarded the date. The letter from Gant had said it was six months since he had put Florence and Annie into the parson's care, and it was presumably shortly before that happened that the crime took place. That meant somewhere around June 1879.

He went through scores of boxes, examining the records from that month. Finally, after forty minutes, with the time ticking away, he found it.

> Florence Emily Hawes. Found fugitive from local magistrate, Watkins JP. Suspected in homicide of her lawful husband, one James Hawes, Turnglass House, Ray, Mersea, Essex.

That was interesting. Watkins had declared his daughter fugitive and asked for aid in recovering her. He had told Simeon nothing of this. A weak man, Watkins, a man who would not even stand by his own actions.

> Florence Emily Hawes also known to

The sound of a key being pushed into the lock alerted him. He thrust the lid back on the box, pushed it into place on the shelf and slipped the file inside his coat. The clerk hustled in, evidently out of breath and irritated. His house must have been close by. For now, Simeon was hidden by a wall of shelves, but would not be for long. He had little choice but to brazen it out.

Harrison was pulling off a greatcoat as Simeon stomped towards him.

'Why did you leave your door unlocked?' he demanded angrily. The other man whirled around, astonished by Simeon's presence and at a loss for words. 'As Mr Gant's representative, I will be making a full report of this!' he warned darkly as he made his way out. 'For God's sake, make sure you lock it next time.' He slammed the door behind him and stalked up the corridor.

He heard the man look out. 'Sir?' was called at his back, but he ignored it, climbed the stairs and went quickly out a side exit from the building. He found a narrow passageway that led out onto Covent Garden market, and wound through the throng to make sure he could not be followed or accosted. After a while he stopped, looked behind him, decided it was safe, and set down in a gaslit coffee house in Floral Street. He opened the file.

'Can I offer you something, sir? Something nice?' A woman was leering over him. She nodded in the direction of the corner. Two young girls were shivering in hired dresses and showing a lack of cleavage due to lack of nourishment.

'Coffee, please,' he replied. 'That's all.'

She shrugged and went to fetch it.

He looked down to where he had left off reading the file. There were just a few more lines.

Florence Emily Hawes also known to have aided and abetted removal of known prostitute from place of asylum decreed by Mr Gant on previous occasion. Prostitute name Annie White.

Strange. Why would Florence be 'abetting the removal' of John White's sister? His mind bubbled with possible explanations, few making sense, but he quelled them to read on.

Florence Emily Hawes and Annie White entrusted into care of Dr Oliver Hawes, clergyman, to be returned to native parish to stand trial.

It was frustrating. The record explained nothing of why Florence had absconded to London and taken Annie White out of an unspecified 'place of asylum decreed by Mr Gant'.

He glanced up at the two streetwalkers in the corner. One was blanched, her eyes half-dead. Probably the clap. He invited her over. She started to walk, but the landlady instantly appeared.

'She don't come free. A crown,' the woman demanded. The girl looked embarrassed.

Simeon slid the coin across the table and the procuress was satisfied, retiring behind a bar stocked with fly-flecked meat pies.

He pulled out a chair for the girl and she sat. 'How are you feeling today?' he asked.

'Well, thank you, sir.' It was surely more formal speech than she would normally have spoken to a client.

'You look unwell.'

'I am quite clean, sir. Certified.'

He was fully aware of the advertisements in newspapers for 'Mrs such-and-such's nunnery' where one of the rooms was occupied by a doctor who would examine the girls before every client visit. He was certain the employ would pay better than his own practice. Such houses were only frequented by gentlemen who paid in paper – indeed, often the very judges and police commissioners who had spent that day shutting down the bordello's lower-class competition.

'I am a doctor.' She visibly stiffened. 'What's wrong?'

'Begging your pardon, sir, but I don't think I'm the right girl for you.'

'No, no, I don't want to be your client. I think you are unwell and I can help.'

She stood and retreated to the corner, where her friend stared at him aggressively. The landlady came over.

'What's this?' she demanded.

'I told her I'm a doctor and I think she's unwell.'

'Doctor?'

'Yes.'

Her expression tightened. 'Then you're not welcome.'

First, he was surprised; then he was curious. 'Why?' he asked.

'Some bad sorts are doctors.'

'I know, I've met some. But what are you referring to?'

She glared at him for a few moments. 'Some cut up girls,' she said.

'What on earth do you mean?'

She hefted herself up. 'Just down the road. They say he was a doctor anyway. Handy with a knife. Enjoyed himself, they say.' She sniffed, then dropped his coin in front of him.

'Tell her to present herself at the Royal Free Hospital. They'll treat her,' he said. He knew the men there. They would see her as well as they could without payment.

She glared at him again.

He took up the file and left. Out on the street, he glanced along the road where the woman had indicated some girls had been 'cut up'. They were right beside the flower market. Such beauty and such ugliness within a spit of each other.

It was too early to head to the location Florence had told him could provide an insight into some of the secrets held at Turnglass House, and so he had to kill some time. He set out on foot through the market. There were stalls selling every flower and every spice that could be obtained throughout the Empire, the latter stacked in baskets piled with golden, dun-coloured or bright green dust. It was, he realized, probably the first time he had been to Covent Garden and really looked through the market. From there, he wandered along Floral Street. There were more girls on that street, some beckoning him, but he kept his mind on the wares in the shop windows.

His feet naturally turned towards King's College

Hospital to the east. He walked along the Strand, past his home in Grub Street, under the shadow of St Paul's dour dome, stopping to buy a fizzing soda in Paternoster Square that he drank leaning against some iron railings. He peered up at a window wherein he was sure his rival for medical research funding, Edwin Grover, was hard at work over his tables and calculations. Grover's work was not entirely without merit, no, but it had no real application. Simeon discarded the dregs of his drink and went on to the hospital.

After twenty minutes wandering through its wards, he found his lodging-mate, Graham, among the beds for those who had broken limbs. He was examining a man's leg. The man, a vintner to guess by his florid face, was wincing in pain, although Graham was paying little attention.

'Simeon, old man!' Graham proclaimed, dropping the limb to the stiff sheet. Its owner showed intense relief. 'Back so soon?'

'Just for the day. There's something I need to find out.'

'Ah, more research.'

'Indeed.'

'So, what's the scenario in Essex?'

Simeon outlined the strange situation. His friend seemed, by turns, astonished and aghast. 'My God,' he said. 'I thought it was just some ill parson.' The man on the bed had let his mouth fall open in amazement.

'Oh, I wish it were that. But I fear there's much worse behind it.'

'Well, be careful. It seems you're poking about in some dangerous corners.'

Simeon agreed and they chatted for a while, until it was late enough to resume his journey.

It was a grim evening in London as he stepped out of the hospital. The smoke from ten thousand home fires had mixed grittily with the sheet fog rolling up the Thames. The blend had a vile green hue – like pea soup, the locals joked as they spat out thick sputum. Aristocratic ghosts were stumbling through the smog in their toppers and tie studs while youthful street sweepers cleared a barely visible path through the horse dung for them.

Hailing a cab, Simeon told the driver to take him to Limehouse.

'You sure, sir?' the cabbie asked. 'Rough 'round there. Gentleman like you.'

'Thank you. I know what I'm doing.'

'If you say so.'

The driver whipped up the horses and they clipped through the smoky mist. Simeon reached into the pocket of his travelling cloak and drew out the flower-carved pipe that he had found in the secretary cabinet at the house. In preparation for the task ahead, he broke it in two.

Chapter 13

Within the Hansom, Simeon covered his face with a muffler, hoping to breathe in less of the smog stink. There was no point looking out the window, he could hardly see to the other side of the cab. On the way, he thought about the teachings of the new psychologists and how some believed that in each of us our base desires fight against our conscious morality. He had never believed in wickedness in the way that religious men, such as his uncle, believed in it. He thought actions were right or wrong, for sure – who did not think that? – but not that they laid an indelible stain on one's character.

'I'll set you down here, sir,' the driver called down.

'I have no idea where we are,' he replied.

'Well, that makes for two of us. Only I daren't go further 'cause we're as like to end up in the river. Can't see me own hand in front of me face.'

Simeon relented, unbolted the door and jumped out. The beams from the carriage lamps stared into the smog, turning it yellow, but penetrating no further than the doctor could reach. It was strange to end up in London's docklands. He had been called there a few times – it was outside his normal patch, but occasionally he had heard of a particular case that could have helped his research. This time he was going not as a doctor but in the guise of a client of the worst kind of house.

Somewhere close, he heard two people – women – arguing. 'Give it back, bitch. Give it.'

'It's mine! He gave it me!'

'Give it, or I'll do you!'

Simeon turned his head away from the sound.

'You sure you want leaving here, sir?' the cabbie called one last time.

'I'm sure.'

'Your funeral.'

He hoped that the phrase would be just a form of words, rather than literal truth. In Limehouse, it could easily be the latter. He handed up some money and the driver tapped his whip to his hat.

Simeon's feet swished through running water. Something scuttled over his boot and squealed as he kicked it away. So many creatures around him. All as sinful as they were unseen. Well, he was going to a place where fresh sins blotted out the old.

Men throughout London had succumbed to the poppy pipe. Of course, most opium was now grown in the British Empire, in India, and shipped to China for consumption, much against the wishes of the Chinese Emperor, yet it was the Chinese who ran the houses in London.

And even though it was a decade since the Pharmacy Act had stopped everyone from barbers to ironmongers selling opium, the fancy of the age would not let it pass into history – there were a dozen poppy houses in this street and the next. Calling in, three or four politely told him they did not sell pipes, however; a few more said they did, but none quite like this one; and one owner took exception to any questions at all and bade Simeon leave without delay.

After the last rejection, he felt his way along the damp cobbles, from time to time catching sight of hulking shades through the river-bound fog. Huge screw steamers bound for Canton or California. California – that place that had occupied the thoughts of the inmates of Turnglass House. He had, in actual fact, thought sometimes of going to that state himself. The gold rush of thirty years earlier had made some men very rich and all men avaricious, but what it represented to Simeon was opportunity without the stifling constraint of the medical establishment or men's petty minds. And opportunity was what he wanted above all. Just the chance to make his mark.

And then he found the place for which he was searching.

It looked to have once been a seaman's mission. Its red roof pitched over a squat building of misshapen yellow bricks with two rows of small windows, while a wide entrance was flanked by two black sailors who nodded to him as if passing an acquaintance in the street. And above them was a red lantern, just as Florence had said.

Even before he had requested admission, a tiny Malay man hurried him in, overjoyed to have a customer, it seemed, and pushed him through an inner door into a big open hall. He found the walls were lined with bunk beds crowded with gaunt faces; while a thick blue haze drifted from mouths and spurted from pipes bubbling over little lamps.

Most of the faces were men whose wan features suggested that they were past the middle of life, but Simeon knew well how the poppy aged a man, so that you should take ten years from an opium-smoker's looks to reckon his real tally. Neither poverty nor war nor disease could wear someone down like the pipe could. They became bestial faces then, turned into chattering monkeys, all humanity sucked away.

'Noooo ... I'll ... I'll ... pay. I have ...' one of the few woman burbled as she was hauled from her bed. Her gaze fixed on Simeon as he walked. 'Sir, will you lend me ... Lend me a ...' She fell to her knees before him.

He bent down and took her pulse. 'Calm yourself,' he said. Her heartbeat was slow but regular. He took two coins from his pocket and handed them to the Malay. 'One for you, one for a cab to take her to the nearest doss-house.'

The Malay bowed and took the coins, propelling the

woman towards the street. Simeon would have to start looking after his purse more closely; the trip was becoming expensive.

There was precious little heat in the vast room, but what warmth there was came from a sparse fireplace at the end, around which a dozen bodies were dozing or lying unconscious. One or two were warming their bones before returning to the world outside, having exhausted their persons and their pockets. One staggered away, muttering to himself, 'Who am I now? Who am I now?' He fell onto an empty bunk and snatched at the pipe there, putting it to his lips and sucking hard, wholly unaware that it was cold and empty. A man wearing only trousers came along, grabbed the other man's ankles and wrenched him out. 'My pipe,' he growled in an accent Simeon could not begin to place.

Simeon's vision fell on a man on a bunk. Unlike the others, the man was not smoking his opium, but sipping from a green bottle. He had a hare lip, which was causing the liquid to dribble down his chin.

'Would you like to try a little, sir?' the man asked. He grinned, to show a maw devoid of teeth. Yet his voice was educated. A university man, by the sound of it. 'The lower-life people in this establishment like to chase the dragon. Me, I prefer to drown it in brandy.'

'So I see,' Simeon replied. 'But laudanum is just as addictive, you must understand.'

'Oh, oh, you need not tell me, sir. I am a full fellow of the Royal College of Surgeons.'

Simeon sighed. He had seen other brother medics

succumb to their own drugs. There was something especially tragic about a man who predicted his own rotten fate and still fell into it. 'Then I advise you to take a care: look to your training and consider the dangers of opium, as well as the pleasures.'

'But I do take a care,' the man insisted, more wildly.

'And how may that be?'

The fallen surgeon was more addled than he had first appeared, Simeon realized. 'How? Just so!' He took a long spoon from within his grimy shirt, inserted it into the bottle and stirred the drink vigorously. 'You must stir it well. Otherwise, the opium falls to the bottom and the dose grows as you eke through the bottle. You must.' He took another swig and offered it to Simeon. 'Try for yourself, sir.'

'I thank you, but no.' His thoughts were depressed for a moment. This man should have been curing the near-dead souls who surrounded him, not joining them. If he could be drawn out of this hell-mouth, he might still shake off the addiction and return to his former profession – although there would be horrendous shaking and sweating consequences for his body as the opium left its conquered land. 'Is there anyone you would like me to contact on your behalf? Family or friends? Maybe some of your old colleagues could help.'

'Help? Help how?' The man seemed alarmed. 'I am more than happy, I assure you, sir. I am delirious! I wish to stay! I wish to stay!' He grabbed Simeon's shirt and had to have his fingers gently eased away.

'You can stay if you like, sir.'

'I do! I must!'

There was no point arguing with the already dead, Simeon wearily told himself.

'You are not like most of my customers.' The voice was young and female. The accent Chinese. He turned to face her and beheld a young woman in the habit of a nun.

'You are not like most of the women in Limehouse,' he replied.

'Do you mean this?' She plucked at her wimple. 'I was brought up by the Holy Sisters of Penance in Canton, sir. My heart will always be with them. A pipe I can fetch you.'

'I have a pipe, but it's broken and I would like it replaced.' He drew it from his pocket and showed it.

She took the pipe and examined closely its two severed halves. 'Ivory and terracotta is unusual. Most men like the porcelain.' Her eyes invited his. 'The smoke is warmer. That is why.'

'Is this pipe yours?'

Her voice was like honey as she replied. 'I made this pipe myself. It was mine. Now it is yours.'

'You recognize it?' She delicately traced her finger along the pipe, along the stem of the carved flowers, and winced when her finger came to the break in the ivory. She nodded. 'Then this must be the place my brother came,' he said.

'It must be.'

'Maybe you remember him?'

'Maybe I remember many men.'

'He is different. A parson. Oliver Hawes.'

162

She paused, rolling the name on her tongue. 'I do not know him. But I know the pipe. This pipe was bought by a man by another name.'

'Who?' She stood quite still before leading the way into a room at the rear. It was full of the style of her homeland. Pink silks wafted over stools and tiny porcelain figures of animals were arranged on a mantelpiece. It was infused with the scent of jasmine. 'Who?' Simeon asked again. He placed a bright guinea coin on the table. Yes, he would have to watch his purse very closely.

The woman opened a green jade box containing a neat row of cigarettes. On each, there was a long brown stain up the middle of the paper that said they contained more than tobacco.

'Thank you, but no.'

She lifted one and lit it, allowing the smoke to stretch up to the ceiling, before opening another box. It proved to be filled with drawing materials, and she extracted a pot of purple ink that sat beside three pens arranged impossibly neatly in order of thickness of nib. She selected the smallest, dipped it in the ink and curled it across a leaf of paper. Simeon waited. The nib was dipped again, and another curving line appeared. Again and again ink was added, until a face emerged. It was a European face with round eyes and a strong nose, although the life of its artist animated it such that the man wore the clothing of an oriental emperor. And yet the face was familiar.

'This man is the one you are looking for,' she said.

'What is his name?'

'His name is Mr Tyrone.'

Simeon once more heard his uncle crying out, in his death throes, for Tyrone.

'What do you know of him?'

'Know of him? We do not ask many questions of our patrons,' she told him.

'I'm sure. But there will be something.'

She held out her palm, dimly pink in the yellow from the oil flames and the orange from the fire. He placed his last bright crown within it and it closed on the metal.

'Many of our customers have something they are missing,' she said. 'Mr Tyrone struck me as a man missing everything. Do you understand my meaning?'

'I believe I do.'

'I often feel sorry for my customers. But I do not think anything could make me feel sorry for Mr Tyrone. You cannot feel sorry for a man who is hollow.'

A hollow man. Simeon had treated patients like that. Men at the end of hard, scrabbling lives who seemed to have died long ago and only their bodies were moving and breathing and eating. This man, Tyrone, who was at the heart of all that had befallen Florence and the Hawes family, was of their number.

'I should like to meet him.'

'He is a man who can cause trouble. Why would I help you find him?'

'Because you don't want him coming back here.'

She paused, then, from nowhere, she produced a small bell and shook it. A part of the pink-papered wall slid away – a doorway deliberately obscured from the uninitiated – and a dark, heavy-set man approached. The patroness addressed him while still gazing on Simeon.

'When did you last see Mr Tyrone?' she asked.

'Tyrone?' The man's accent was as Irish as the name he growled. 'That bastard still owes for services. Haven't seen him for a year or more.'

'And what services did you render him?' Simeon enquired.

The woman nodded to her assistant, telling him to speak.

'Sent a man to help him recover some property of his, down St George's Fields. Seemed easy enough from what he said. Turned out to be a rum bash – not what he said it was. You see him? You tell him that Frank at the Red Lantern hasn't forgotten him.'

'I think that will be all we can help you with,' his mistress said.

Outside the building, Simeon began walking in search of a cab. Through his thoughts fell Tyrone, the poppy pipe, John White's corpse laid out, *The Gold Field* and Florence imprisoned behind glass. They all tumbled like grains of sand through Turnglass House's hourglass weather vane.

He passed along the edge of the dock. In the water, he caught sight of a house behind him. The reflection rippled. And as he watched it move, disintegrate and reassemble by the second, a thought struck him like an arrow. It was a searing realization, a sudden comprehension about the killing of Dr Oliver Hawes. He, Simeon,

had been looking at the death from the wrong angle –
reflected, indeed, in the dark mirror that bound one end
of the man's book-filled domain. Simeon knew now how
the parson had died.

Chapter 14

He returned at speed to Ray with his mind a riotous theatre. Actors seemed to be running onto the stage, shouting out a confusion of lines, dying, stabbed by wooden knives, and returning in different guises.

When he reached the house, Mrs Tabbers came to him in the parlour and offered him a fish stew. He set aside the question, instead posing one of his own. 'How long would the parson eke out one of his barrels of brandy?'

'A whole barrel? Oh, he wasn't a big drinker, sir. Could be a year with ease.'

'I thought so,' he replied. 'I would probably do the same. No fish stew, thank you.'

She gave him a bemused look and took her leave. He

stared out the window over the wild landscape of Ray, illuminated by the house's gaslight. His mind was settling, and yet the truth he now knew was as bleak as the scene outside.

And is this what brought it all into being? he asked himself. *Men and women on a blasted turf. Wouldn't it drive anyone to a blasted mind?*

He called for Peter Cain. The man came with his hands filthy and a shovel in his grip. 'I been buryin' that dead foal. No use fer lame animals. Wan' ter help me dig him in?' he said insolently. Simeon sent him to bring Watkins immediately, and then went up to the library. Florence was sitting at the small octagonal table, upon which sat the little glass model of the house that held them all, its three human figurines waiting behind the coloured doors of the upper floor like actors ready to play their parts. There was a fire in the grate, and the light of its red flames danced across the yellow silk dress Simeon had picked out for her. She sang a snatch from the hymn once more, '*Help of the helpless, oh, abide with me.*'

Simeon felt the urge to pull an atlas from one of the bookshelves, opening it at a map of the Americas. He placed the tip of his index finger on California and tapped it on a headland that bore no label, but that he knew would one day be named Point Dume.

'Don't go, Simeon,' she said softly.

'Why not?'

'It won't end well. Tragedy for you and your family.' She ran her palms over the glass model she had made.

'And how do you know that it will end badly?'

'Oh, Simeon, we both do. It's all in *The Gold Field*. It won't take much: a spark of ambition here, a flicker of wrath there. The sins rack up until the whole house burns. It's the dust in the air; it makes the blood foul.'

When Watkins finally arrived, around ten o'clock, Simeon offered him a drink, which he accepted.

'And now, Mr Watkins, may I have the book?'

'What book?' The magistrate stared at his feet.

Florence lifted the three figurines from the miniature of Turnglass House, setting them down, one by one, in front of it.

'You know quite well what book. Oliver Hawes's journal.'

'I have no idea—'

'Please don't waste my time, sir. I know you took it. And I know why.'

Watkins seemed ashamed still, but summoned a little strength. 'Do you, sir? Then please explain how you came to that conclusion.'

'I will.' He paused to gather his thoughts. 'I have been unable to understand how Oliver Hawes came to die.' Florence knocked one of the figurines over. It rolled a little on the table top. 'It could have been an infection, but if so which one? None that I recognized. And nobody else appeared to have it. You're all hardy souls here. And there was no sign of serious internal disease when I performed an autopsy. No, I eventually came around to Dr Hawes's own hypothesis: that he was poisoned last month.' He ignored Watkins's apparent shock. 'But again, the question of how had me utterly stumped. He ate the same food as Cain and Mrs Tabbers and neither of them displayed any symptoms. It could have been one of them, of course, but quite why they would want to make themselves destitute by murdering their employer would be hard to fathom. And even if they did, there would be easier methods – they could have smothered him in his sleep and no one would have been any the wiser.'

Watkins looked like he wanted to raise an objection but could not think of one. Simeon continued. 'There was only one source of food or drink that Dr Hawes alone consumed: his nightly nip of brandy. The barrel was new the day before the onset of his sickness, but he became increasingly ill for more than a week after he stopped drinking it at my direction; and in addition, we tested the barrel on Cain's poor dog – apart from getting the poor mutt blootered, it had no effect. I also tested it myself later at Colchester Royal and it was quite harmless. No, the barrel had not been poisoned. Indeed, nobody poisoned Oliver Hawes last month.'

'Then what are you getting at?' Watkins demanded, at last rousing himself.

'It is simple, sir.'

'Then tell me!'

'Somebody poisoned him a year ago.' He felt little elation. He was angry that it had all come to this.

'A year ago? Impossible. Who?'

'Your daughter, Mr Watkins.' It was a relief to say the words and to look at her as he spoke them.

'Florence,' Watkins gasped. The game was up, it seemed.

She swept all the glass figures to the floor, leaving only the transparent house.

'Yes. Florence.' His eyes remained locked on her. 'She poisoned Oliver Hawes more than a year ago, the last time she was let out of her glass prison cell.'

Watkins collapsed back into his chair. 'But how could . . .' He trailed off.

Slowly, to the beat of a funeral step, she lifted her hands and brought the palms together. *Clap. Clap. Clap.* 'Bravo, Simeon. You are a sharp little knife.' Her voice sounded like one. 'I wonder what else you have learned or guessed.'

He gazed at her. 'Since you ask, I have a strong suspicion regarding the death of John White and how the inmates of this house were involved in it. How James was entwined in it. And then there is John's sister, Annie, whom you sought out in London. Where is she now? That's a question we need answered.'

Watkins burst out again, 'You think something untoward happened to her too?'

Simeon did not turn away from the woman behind the glass. 'Yes, I do. Don't you, Florence?' But he did not elaborate. Watkins would always be three steps behind his daughter. 'What happened after you found her?' She beamed at him. 'It's all in Hawes's journal, isn't it?' He addressed Watkins. 'And that's why you stole it. To protect your daughter. Something you had failed to do previously. Because its contents would have led me to the conclusion that Florence is guilty of murder.' Watkins let out a small moan and drank down his glass. His daughter laughed lightly. But Simeon's mind was fixed still on the

171

book and nothing else. 'I presume she told you of its contents after Oliver's death.' The magistrate made no demur this time. 'Then for God's sake, let's end this charade. Give me the journal!'

'I . . .'

'I say we give it to him, Father,' she said, her voice less muffled by the glass than of late. 'What do you care now? What do I care?' She waved her hand without concern.

'Send Cain to your house for it,' Simeon ordered him.

'There is no need,' Watkins mumbled. 'It never left the room.'

'*What?*' Simeon was outraged. It was still here! All that time spent pondering over its location.

Watkins wiped sweat from his brow. 'I was afraid you would catch me when I ran. So I hid it here safely, in the dark. That way, you wouldn't get your hands on it.'

Simeon took a moment to consider the information. The man had hidden it in the room, but where could he have placed it such that Simeon could not have come across it by chance? Oh, one place only. Simeon turned to the glass.

'Give me the book, Florence,' he said. 'I want to read of the second life of Oliver Hawes.'

She placed her hand on the miniature glass house on the table, tipping it onto its side. 'Do you think we are masters of our own fates, Simeon? Oh, I see that you do. Well, you are wrong. We are but the playthings of others.' Her voice was low, tangled up in the Sargasso weed once more. 'A second life, you call it.'

'Yes. That's what it was, wasn't it?'

'Perhaps.'

She went to the shelves that lined the rear wall of her cell, reached up to run her finger along the highest shelf and stopped it on a slim red volume with gold lettering on the spine. She could have taken it through to her private apartment, where it would have been wholly out of sight, but she had evidently enjoyed the fact that Simeon had seen it hour in, hour out, and yet never *seen* it. She pulled it down and stepped to the small hatch through which her meals were supplied – no doubt that was how Watkins had got it to her – and her pale hand pushed it through. For the second time, their fingertips touched and held for a moment, before she slowly drew back into her own world.

'Why did you keep it from me? You wanted me to read it before.'

'It was Father's doing. He came to me and begged me to keep the full facts from you. It was more to save his own reputation than my neck, but I relented.' Watkins seemed to fold even more into himself.

Simeon let that go. He was desperate to know the contents of the journal, those that he had not yet read. He turned the book over and opened the back cover to once more reveal the secret journal of Oliver Hawes. He continued whence he had left off.

19 May 1879

That good man Tyrone found me this evening. I was at the Bricklayer's Arms in Colchester, having been to speak to the Dean about financial matters. I was eating some leek soup and reading a

173

treatise on poverty in the Church. 'Hello,' I said, looking up. There were many other people in the saloon and I was sure most of them should have been in the public bar.

'I've been looking for you,' he said to me.

'Oh, why is that?'

He sat down. 'I'm famished,' he declared. And he took the spoon right out of my hand and drank some of my soup. 'I have been busy, that is why.'

'Busy doing what?' I was annoyed that he had taken the spoon from me, but I let it pass because I had an inkling that he had something important to say.

'Checking. Looking into things. And I'll tell you something, my friend, I believe we are missing — well, you are missing — a trick to play.'

'To what do you refer?'

'Something tells me that you are not a free man.'

'Not free? Absurd,' I replied. I must admit I was a little irritated by his insolent tone. 'Look at my wrists, do you see chains upon them? Observe the door — is it locked? Can I stand and walk right through it and mount my horse to ride home?'

'No, no chains on your wrists.' Here he leaned in and I could smell something cadaverous on his breath. 'And yet . . .' He sat back on the rough bench. I supposed he would say more. But he waited. And I realized right away that he had, indeed, hit upon a problem that had confounded my brain for too many years. A question about the freedom of will granted to us by our Heavenly Father.

'And yet?' I prompted him.

'And yet you cannot. Because it is against all that the Scripture tells us.' And there it was indeed.

'Do tell.' I pushed the bowl away. It no longer interested me.

'You wish for what I have.'

'You do not strike me as a rich man.'

'Confound my cash money!' he snarled. 'You want what I truly have: the freedom to grab and blow hard. The freedom to make merry as I will.'

He was becoming quite animated on the subject. 'And what makes you believe I would countenance any such addition to my life?'

'I've seen you read the Scriptures day in, day out.'

'I have not seen you,' I said, slightly surprised by the assertion.

'I sat at the back of the church.'

'I see.' I was unsure whether to believe him.

'And each time, I caught something in your eye or the turn of your mouth. For each one of those deadly sins or commandments, there was . . .'

'Was what?'

He avoided the question infuriatingly. 'I've sailed around the world. You have the look of the sailor as he nears a new land – a desperation to leap ashore and savour what he can.'

I took a sip of my small beer and gazed at him over its rim. 'Indeed?' And I relaxed. 'Oh, but you are making a mock of me, a poor country parson.'

'Poor! Hah! We can be agreed that you are certainly none of that. A country parson, yes, but poor, oh no. I cannot allow that.'

Yes. This one had depth. I stood and left the saloon bar. I knew that he would follow.

'Your speech I find interesting. Not that I will act upon it, but for now I am curious as to the endpoint of your argument.'

'You'll see that soon enough,' he said somewhat cryptically. 'There's something I've wanted to show you for some time. The time's come.'

'I am a busy man. I cannot run on fools' errands.'

'True, true,' he conceded. 'But this you will benefit by.'

I realized that we had walked to a wealthy part of the town I had only entered once or twice at the invitation of the Dean or other such luminaries. I was wearing my travelling coat and wrapped it tighter to keep warm. I have always been a martyr to the diseases of other people.

Tyrone was in front of me and he went up to a house that had lights on. He knocked and it was opened by a butler in full livery.

'Yes?' this man enquired.

'I've heard of this house,' Tyrone told him. I thought it strange behaviour and was ready to apologize for my companion's gruffness.

'Have you now? What have you heard?'

'Oh, stand aside, man,' Tyrone ordered him. I was somewhat taken aback. I had thought this to be the house of a friend of his. Even men such as him – I had it in my mind that his morality was open to question, despite his regular attendance at Holy Communion – have friends.

'I will stand aside only when you tell me who sent you,' the butler insisted.

'Sent me? Sent me, you say? This gentleman sent me.' It took a moment for me to realize what he was getting at: he had put his hand in his pocket book and pulled out a whole guinea. Such wealth some men have to give away! The wind was very strong then and it muffled a bit what Tyrone said, but whatever the precise words were, the man stood back and we were across the threshold.

What a surprising sight it was inside. It looked as if a prince was in residence. All around were plush leather armchairs – far better than those in my library – and love seats and potted plants.

And a wide marble staircase leading up. 'Well, don't just stand there with your mouth agape like the Colne estuary,' Tyrone said to me. And he laughed. 'Come in. We'll taste the delights.'

There was drink to be had, I could see that, because there were bottles and glasses on tables, but to what else he was referring I could not tell.

He went to one of the tables and took up a decanter of what seemed to be sherry.

'No excise paid on this, I'll say,' he muttered.

'I am sure you are correct there.'

And then something made me look up, up the staircase: steps on the marble. Three young women were tripping lightly, led by an older dame. They were dressed for an evening at the opera or such and they were all quite beautiful and beautified. Poets would have had them looking like birds.

'Good evening, gentlemen,' the older one said. She wore attractive stones around her neck and her dress positively floated as she walked.

Tyrone sat on a settle and motioned to me to do the same. I felt a little unsure, but did as he instructed me. 'Good evening, madam,' he said. 'I would have some entertainment.'

'That we can offer.' She looked at me and my clerical garb. It upset her not a bit. I think it might even have tickled her. She waved her hand towards the younger ladies. 'Isabella, Clarice and Amelia are new to this, and yet I know they will provide pleasure.'

'New to this?' Tyrone burst out. 'Ha! That's a good one. I had the yellow-haired one last month and she was fine for the use. I'll have her again, I think.' And then he stood up and made towards the young lady at the back.

'And for you, sir?' She addressed me without my divine title, defrocking me.

Before I could speak, Tyrone spoke for me. 'I go in his place,' he informed her. She looked to me and her delicate brow arched. I made no reply and she took that as consent.

'As you will, sirs. Go with the gentleman, Isabella.'

She began to ascend the stairs and Tyrone followed. 'Wait,' he said. 'I don't like the name Isabella.'

'You do not, sir?' the procuress enquired.

'No. I want it changed.'

'What would you like it to be?'

Tyrone said nothing, but looked to me.

'Florence,' I said.

'Florence, sir?' the girl asked. She had a light voice, from the north of our country.

'Yes,' I said. 'You are to be Florence.'

Chapter 15

Simeon paused reading and looked up. How strange it was. Florence seemingly read his mind.

'A hidden journal, a hidden man,' she said.

'He was.' He read on.

25 May 1879

Parish business took me to Colchester again and I ate at the Bricklayer's Arms. When I arrived, Tyrone was there, the only one at the inn.

'Dr Hawes,' he greeted me cheerily. Indeed, he was cheerier and more vivacious than usual. And I guessed why. One of our village girls, Annie White, the daughter of an oyster fisher, was pouring

his ale. She is a plain thing if you ask me, but I am sure she serves the purpose that most of the menfolk in these parts would put her to. 'You know Annie, I am sure.'

'Of course. How are you, Annie?'

'I am well, Parson. Thankye for askin'.'

I often find the obsequious nature of the poor – form without substance – grating. 'And your mother is well?'

'She is, sir.'

'Well, I will take some mutton stew.'

'I was just telling little Annie how she would do well on the stage,' Tyrone continued. I was sure she would. No doubt every slattern could make a living being gawped at by unwashed men if she had the inclination. 'Would you not like to see her on the stage in Colchester? The Theatre Royal. Or London!'

The girl's gaze turned quite glassy. I could see she was dreaming of a life quite apart from the Hard.

I smiled indulgently. 'As a man of the Book, such things are rather beyond my gamut,' I said. And I lowered my voice for her. 'The Church rather frowns on such places, seeing them as cauldrons for all sorts of irreligious practice.' She giggled at that.

Tyrone and I took a table and talked of minor matters – the people in the inn, my plans for a little holiday on the south coast. And then he steered the conversation around to the house we had visited on the previous occasion.

'It is like supping at G—d's own table,' he said. 'And no sin, I'm sure.'

'Are you?' I said, with some scepticism.

Yet, strange as it seems, he came back with genuine religious arguments for it being so. As he pointed out, the Bible makes a point of stating how the patriarchs of the Hebrews enjoyed relations with their many womenfolk. Are they not held up as models for our behaviour in the absence of more direct exhortations by our Saviour?

'But such relations are within sanctified marriage,' I disputed.

'Ah, but who is delegated by G—d to perform such sanctification? His representative.' He meant me, of course. 'The priest is the mortal man who declares marriage, doesn't he? So what is sanctified is within his gift. There is nothing to stop him bestowing such gifts on other priests — doesn't the Lord encourage it? — so there is nothing to stop him bestowing that sanctity on his own self.'

I did not like being tutored by a man who . . . in fact, as I considered it, I realized I barely even knew what he did by way of employ, something in the way of a merchant sailor, I thought. But he had theological strength behind his argument.

'True enough, yet a cleric must also pay heed to the great authorities.'

'Ah, but how did those authorities become authorities themselves? Why, by considering and testing,' he countered.

I thought this over too. Again, there was force there. We walked out to talk more.

'Lot of ruffians around tonight,' he said, checking over his shoulders and peering into the doorways.

'More than usual?'

'For sure. I saw a man beaten to within an inch of his life this evening.'

'For what offence?' I asked, shocked.

'Nothing. Looked at a man the wrong way. Criminal times we live in.'

'That is for certain.' I had myself been concerned, having read frequent reports in the newspapers of needless brutality.

'Yes. In fact, I was thinking. You should carry this,' he said. I looked down at his palm. Lying across it was an evil-looking dagger. My mouth fell open.

'What need have I of that?' I demanded. 'I do not shed men's blood.'

'But you have to be ready to stop someone else shedding yours. And there's enough of them around these parts as have the want and the time to do it.'

I sighed unhappily. Once more, he had a point. And there is no sin in self-preservation – if anything, since suicide is the wilful and ungrateful disregard of the life that G–d has granted us, there is a compunction on us to defend ourselves when others would cut our throats. So, reluctantly, I took the knife. It was a sleek thing, long and slim but with a razor edge. I did not ask to what use he had previously put it. I placed it inside my coat, into a pocket where it fitted snugly.

14 June 1879

I met Tyrone on the Hard. It had been more than two weeks since I had seen him last and I had been looking forward to continuing our conversation; there were some points that I wanted to discuss in his argument that the Hebrew patriarchs should be our model with womenfolk when there is no more direct exhortation from Christ Jesus himself. We were walking to my house and had just come off the Strood.

'Parson!' I heard someone shout at our backs. It was not often that I would hear my honorific cried at my back as I approached my home. And it was not being yelled out in a friendly fashion. 'Parson!' it repeated.

I glanced at Tyrone. His eye met mine darkly.

'Hide yourself,' he said.

'I will do no such thing.'

'All right, you d—mned fool,' he growled. 'I'll be the one to hide.'

I continued on my course without breaking my stride, as if I had not heard the man hailing me. Tyrone slipped from the path and down the side of the creek, onto the mudflats. His mottled black garb made him quite invisible in the dusk to anyone who knew not that he was there. Even I felt his presence more than I saw it.

The thudding step of my pursuer came within earshot. I gave it no heed. He would come, whoever he was — in fact, I had a good idea whom he might be — and I would deal with him as required. There is a reason that we divines are addressed as 'Father'. It is because, like any good parent, we must often dole out remonstrance as much as guidance.

When I could no longer stand the sound of his uneven, beastly tread, I suspended my motion and awaited his appearance.

'Parson!' he barked. I looked him up and down. A heifer in a man's body: heavy and stupid. I cared little for what he was to say, so did not trouble myself to invite it. When he finally reached me, he was huffing and puffing as if he would keel over. When he had recovered a little, during which time I waited patiently for whatever nonsense was due to be spilled from his lips, he straightened up and stared me in the face. 'My sister,' he growled — I was mistaken, he was no heifer, he was a street hound. 'What you did to my sister.'

'I have done nothing to your sister,' I answered him. And it was the utter truth. Anything that had been done to this man's sister — it was now clear to whom he referred — was done by Tyrone, and without instruction from me. My conscience was clear.

'Annie . . . She was to be married.'

183

'Then let her marry,' I said. 'I will happily perform the ceremony myself.'

'She cannot now. She is not clean!'

I was beginning to tire of the conversation. That is hardly a barrier for most of you people. She is probably five times as "clean" as the average bride around these parts. Now, if you will excuse me, I have a sermon to write.'

And that was when he made his great error. He grabbed my frock-coat as I recovered my path to the house and wrenched me back. I almost toppled from his strength. In these parts, men are bred for toiling the land and drawing in a catch and it is proved in their bulk, not their brains. 'How dare you attack the Church this way!' I upbraided him. My outrage took him aback, and he paused his assault on my person. I could see his slow mind recalling years sat on pews while I or my brother priests taught him right from wrong in the sight of G–d.

But then his animal grimace returned. 'No, Parson. You have ruined her.'

And here he drew something from his jerkin. A rumpled slip of paper, greasy thumbprints upon it. It was a scrap torn from something else. I perused a brief, barely legible missive scrawled upon it.

'Sir. I am very sadd. I wonted for you to be my darlling. I am no good for no man nou. I thot you to be my husbant. Annie.'

I know I should have felt this as a poor thing, but I must confess I simply burst out laughing. 'Fancies country life, does she? Think your slattern sister will make a good parson's wife? Oh, my dear man, you have brightened up my day with your lunacy. But I fear I must leave you to it.' I tried to betake myself away, but he threw his arms around me, caging me and crushing me as if he wanted to squeeze the life right out. My hands were free but next-to-useless against his brawn.

'No, Parson. No.' He was growling like a dog again. 'She has drunk of something now. Something that has sent her to sleep. She does not waken.'

I felt the air leaving my chest, and with every expiration he tightened, so that my lungs could suck in no more. I think he really did mean to suffocate me. As I cast about for aid, I looked into his eyes and saw such hate that I scarcely noticed when his torso began to sag against mine. But in an instant, we changed. Where his body had been sapping mine, suddenly mine was holding his upright. Something warm spread over my hands. I peered down and saw it was blood, gushing from a series of wounds in his side, each made by the long blade in Tyrone's hand. As I watched, White staggered away, and Tyrone, like a Fury, leaped behind him, reached around White's neck and plunged the dagger twice deep into his back. My assailant's body slumped to the ground.

I stood stock still, amazed. But in a moment, I recovered myself. Thank the good Lord for ensuring there was no one in sight.

'I told you to carry a blade,' Tyrone said. 'Now you see why you need it.' He spat on the man at his feet. To my shock, I realized White was still moving, his breathing laboured and rattling. 'Don't fright. I'll deal with him,' Tyrone muttered. I retreated a pace to let him do his work. And as I watched, the man's life became thinner. And then it left him.

'Say nothing,' Tyrone anticipated me. 'This is my work, and will continue to be my work. Stand aside.' He bent down and hefted up my assailant's lifeless body, dragging it on its haunches into the muddy creek. I noted I had a fair degree of blood on my person that I would have to wash away. I could hardly give my garb to my housekeeper. I watched as Tyrone pulled the corpse further across the mud and into the parts that are like quicksand, where anything will sink completely out of sight. Tyrone's coat masked them both, but I fancied I saw John's hand slip down into the dirt. And that was the last anyone ever saw of him.

Tyrone came back to me and laughed. 'You'll need this later,' he said. And he slapped to my chest the letter – if you can call it that – that the girl had written. 'I'll see to this man's boat. It will look like he capsized.'

'Do be careful,' I said. He had thrust the letter to my breast just where a spot of my assailant's blood had soaked my shirt, and it was now seeping into the edge of the letter. I wiped the liquid away. I had an inkling how he meant me to use the missive and I was proved right as he outlined his plan to me. It was, I must admit, a subtle one. And at no time would I sinfully bear false witness, I made certain of that.

Yes, I thank our Lord for Tyrone, for sending him to me just when I needed him. Truly, the Great Shepherd's power and beneficence is something to behold.

When he had finished, I retraced my path and headed towards the village on Mersea and the girl's home to see what her brother had spoken of regarding her mental and physical state. I buttoned up my coat and it hid the blood stain quite effectually.

Upon reaching the attractive little cottage, I was led in by a blind old woman – they all seem to share the same mother, her class – to the bed where her daughter lay. I am no physician, but it appeared to me that Annie was heading to the same place whither her brother had already arrived. I placed my hand on her forehead. It was wet and quite cold. I saw the buds of her breasts panting up and down through a thin night slip. A terrible pity to lose such a child from this world, a child with so much to offer, but such is the plan of the Great One.

I blessed her and left. She was in G–d's hands then. Whether she would join Him above us or suffer the torments of the netherworld would be His choice and decision alone. But I was glad I had made the visit, because it meant the rest of my friend's scheme would be all the more predictable.

There are usually one or two ne'er-do-wells sitting around the Hard hoping for a day's work. Where they drift from I have no idea, but they seem to turn up, sit about for a few days, then disappear again, and today I would have use for one of them.

I placed my clerical collar within my pocket and waved one over. He hurried to me, the prospect of a few bob no doubt lighting his fervour. 'Take this letter to the house on Ray immediately and give it to the housekeeper,' I said. I handed over Annie's crumpled note and a small sum for him to spend at the Peldon Rose. I directed him up the Strood and he left at a good pace. I then set myself down to wait for an hour on the shoreline before returning home. I felt the Holy Spirit filling me with jubilation.

As soon as I set foot in the hallway an hour later, I heard them screaming like banshees.

'Who is she, d–mn you?' It was Florence's voice. It was rare – though not unknown – for her to shout loud enough to shake the house in this fashion.

'Have you lost your mind entirely?' James was crying back.
Tyrone really knows his game, I thought.
'If I have, it was when I consented to marriage!'
I betook myself to the study while they continued in the same violent vein, and changed my shirt.

I had spent no more than five minutes reading a treatise on

missions in southern India when my brother burst in. He was clutching a handkerchief to his cheek and it was clear that the linen was soaked red. It reminded me to dispose of my shirt before Tabbers washed it. 'Dash it, Oliver, I have no idea at all what she is referring to,' he said, throwing himself down in a chair.

'Would you like to explain?'

He groaned. 'She has been questioning me about some girl I am supposed to have abused.'

'Did you abuse her?'

'I barely even know the girl. John White's sister. Flo claims to have been delivered of some G—d-awful note claiming I have used this girl, promised to marry her and tossed her aside like a worn pair of shoes. Utter madness.' He booted at a side table. 'Never liked that table. Would be better as firewood,' he said.

'What happened?'

'Flo lobbed a decanter at me. Gin sloshing all over the floor. Good stuff that I had brought over from Flanders last month. Crying shame.'

'And your cheek?'

'Well, it broke, didn't it? Right on my face. Oh, I'll live.' He pulled away the handkerchief, but some of the blood had dried, sticking it to the skin.

It is sometimes a difficult task to remain on the right side of the moral dividing line. But after examining my conscience, I know that I am in the white. I have spoken no false words.

15 June 1879

A more tranquil day. I spent the forenoon on accounts. I have asked the diocese for more funds to employ a sexton, but have received a negative reply. It appears we shall have to delay the repairs to the church roof. James complains of a burning in the gashed flesh.

16 June 1879

I watched over James for a while. He is in pain and angry for it, but being so does him no good. He refused supper. I finished the short treatise on ecumenicism in the Colonies that I was sent by the Anglican Communion Corresponding Society. It was quite instructive.

17 June 1879

Very hot today. James grows ill. His flesh is turning yellow where Florence attacked him. Well, he is in the hands of our Lord and we must bend to His will. He is raving. I repeated my request for a sexton, setting out more reasons for his necessity.

18 June 1879

A tinker has been caught stealing from the Rose. He will be sent to the Assizes for the next quarter-session. James worsens. His condition looks grave.

19 June 1879

There is no wickedness in joy. There is no sin in advantage unsought. I am not Cain, I have slain no brother. And yet he has been slain. He is still breathing, but that will not last long, I am sure. And the perpetrator? His wife. The wound he received at

Florence's hand is green now and drips a foul liquid. The flesh around it is blackened and eaten away. You can see his teeth and bone through it. The doctor for whom we sent — a drunken local fellow little better than the village herbalist — is at a loss, other than to instruct prayer and hopes. I have, indeed, been praying. By turns James sweats and shivers and his lips are cracked dry. He yells from time to time, but thankfully his words are nonsensical.

When I went to him, I held his hand tight and he turned his vision on me. 'Oliver,' he mumbled. 'Be kind to her.'

'I will,' I said.

Tomorrow or the next day, I am certain, I will place my brother in the family crypt and consign him unto G—d's hands.

News also from the village. Annie White has recovered. As soon as she could walk, she left her mother's home, saying only that she was bound for London and would send word when she was able. G—d has stayed her voice from telling tales. Thank Him.

Chapter 16

Simeon turned the page but found nothing more. The leaves of the book were blank from there on. And yet, as he looked more closely, he saw a series of small relics of paper still attached to the spine.

'Where are the other pages, Florence?' he asked. She lifted the glass model. Beneath it was a small pile of pages. Like the journal itself, she had left them in his full sight for days. He had to hand it to her: she was playing her game well. 'Will you give them to me?'

'I might.'

Her intention was clear. 'But you want something in return.'

'How perceptive you are, Simeon! Quite the gallant psychologist.'

'And if I don't provide you with your desire, what happens? You put the lamp flame to them?'

'I think that's likely.'

'So what's the price?'

'The price is my portrait that hangs above the fireplace in the hall.'

He was surprised. 'You want a painting?' It was a curious request – but a cheap one.

'I do.'

The small portrait above the fireplace, of Florence painted some years earlier on an imaginary landscape soaked by the American sun, was easy to lift away from the wall. Cain, who was carrying a bucket of coal through the hall, stared at him, but Simeon affected not to have noticed and took the picture back to the library.

'Ah,' she sighed as she saw him return. 'You are faithful.'

He pushed it through the hatch and she gazed on her younger self. Then she reached for her side table, took a tumbler in her hand and dashed it against the table, breaking it into a dozen pieces. She picked one of the larger shards from the floor and Simeon feared she was going to use it as a weapon against herself. But instead, she stabbed it into the picture at the edge where it met the frame and cut out the canvas.

'What are you doing?' he asked.

'You'll see.'

Behind the picture he saw her real target: a clutch of letters.

'What are those?'

And as he saw them, he saw tears in her eyes. 'These? These are the billets James wrote me. When we were young. I had them put here so that . . .'

'. . . you would always know where they were,' he finished her thought.

And at that, he felt like a voyeur. He departed the room, leaving her to read her old love letters. He could not free her, but he could give her time with her past, with her thoughts and the love she had borne for her husband.

An hour later, he returned. She was standing at the side of her demi-room, leaning against a shelf of books, staring at the line of windows that she could not reach.

'Thank you,' she said. He nodded, accepting the gratitude. Without looking at him, she pushed the remaining pages of the journal through the hatch and he returned to reading Oliver Hawes's unknown history.

20 June 1879

I did indeed inter James today. We were a sad procession – I was sad, myself, that it had come to this. But we are tools of the Lord and must not question.

We stood as one black gathering in the back parlour, where he had been laid out, and I remembered the monograph that I read about the sin-eaters in our part of the country; those wretches who were paid to eat cakes laid out on the body of the deceased in order to take upon themselves all the sins of the newly dead. In the eyes of G–d and the Tempter, those black marks were then transferred from the book of the deceased to the book of that living man and he would have to answer for them on Judgement Day, while the dead man could enter Heaven without hindrance. For sure, it is an atheist's profession. They will get a dread shock when their coffins are cracked open and their souls called up before the final judge.

I fulfilled my priestly duty well, I think, delivering words of deep comfort to all, including Florence. Had it been entirely up to me, I would have allowed her some time to mourn. But Tyrone rightly stated that the immediate aftermath of the funeral would be the most effective time for us to act.

To that end, some hours later I was reading in my library by gaslight. Florence had gone for a walk to clear her head. Tyrone was in the corner, paring his nails in an unpleasant manner.

I had rarely seen such rain even in these soaked parts. Any heavier and Noah himself would have baulked! Tyrone was not the only other man in the room. I had invited Watkins to dine, and he was asleep in the corner, snoring like an African beast. I had filled him with wine and suggested he doze it off here before returning to his house. The servants had been sent home for the night.

'Dirty night,' Tyrone muttered. 'How do you think she will fare?'

'Not well,' I replied, looking up from a volume of commentary on the Pentateuch. 'She is in a fragile state, I am sure.'

'You can be d—mn sure of that.'

'I do wish you would temper your public-bar language when in this house,' I admonished him. 'There is a time and place for it, but this is neither.'

'Sorry,' he grumbled, and he went back to working on his fingernails. 'How long has it been now?' he asked, after a while.

I checked the clock in the corner. 'Nearly an hour. She cannot last for much longer. The chill must be into her bones.' I shut the book and removed my spectacles, so I could better concentrate. The sound of her wailing rose again. It had been angry, then plaintive and was now outwardly threatening.

'Open the doors or I'll skin you, you whoresons!' she was screaming from below. Pebbles rattled against the window pane, but she could find nothing more substantial to throw, nothing to break the glass. And against the sound of the Biblical torrent, I could barely make it out.

'No fine lady, is she?' Tyrone commented. 'Sounds like one of the three-shilling girls in London. Some of them, oh, I could tell you stories! There was one girl, Jessie, who liked it every way. Now, she once—'

I slammed my book down on the table, quite angry. 'I told you to temper these vile stories. If you will be like that, you can leave this house!'

'Oh, pipe down,' he muttered. 'You need me as you need food.'

'I do not!'

I do not like the off-hand way he has been with me of late. After seeing to Florence, I am beginning to suspect I will have to see to Tyrone. It is a dangerous state of affairs when the lackey thinks himself the master.

'Why in the Devil's name you consider that harpy, I'll never know,' Tyrone muttered.

'I want to save her from becoming worse,' I informed him. 'Holy office is anathema to you, is it not?'

'Oh, holy office. That is what you desire from her. Ha!' He cast me a filthy look. 'I'll leave. I don't care what you and she get up to. Treat her like the sailors treat Jessie, for all I care.' And he stomped out of the room. Watkins seemed to stir a little at his leaving, but did not wake.

And then, with an almighty crash, the window bust inwards! A rock had flown right through it, across the room and into the fireplace. Watkins woke with a cry, an amount of the glass showering him. I was sorry, for it quite cracked the tiles around the grate. It was a very unpleasant event.

Without the window between us, her voice seemed to grab hold of the room and shake it about. 'Open the door, you bastards. Open it or I'll beat it down!'

This was followed by a fresh hail of pebbles through the broken window. Some hit Watkins, making him leap out of his skin. 'What is happening?' he cried.

I affected to look as astonished as he. 'I . . . I believe that is your daughter's voice,' I told him.

'Florence? Good G—d, I think it is!'

We stepped cautiously to the broken casement. The rain was lashing through and the curtains billowing in. Once again, I thought of Noah, in the storm of the Flood, tossed on the sea, praying for the survival of his race.

'You animals. Open the door. I'll wring your necks! The Devil help me, I will wring your necks!'

'What in G—d's name is wrong with her?' he asked, frightened. We peeped through the broken glass. She was below, soaked as if she had fallen into the frothing sea in all her clothes. And she was staring back at us with all the hatred of a daemon.

'I see you!' she screamed up. 'I'll do you both with my own hands! Open the door!' Those hands were above her head, reaching up as if to fulfil her promise to strangle us. Then, incredibly, they ceased grabbing at the empty air and instead began grabbing at the stones of the house. She was attempting to climb the very walls, to break in through the window like a monkey. However, she made it no more than a few scrabbled steps up, aided by some vines that held fast to the stone, before falling down to the sodden soil.

Watkins and I shrank back. She was like one of the semi-human creatures in Tyrone's sailor's tales.

'I have never seen her like that!' was all Watkins could exclaim. His words were slurred. His fear at his daughter's state was heightened by the drink that still addled his brain.

'I wish I could say the same,' I replied quietly.

'You mean, it has happened before? She has been like this in the past?' I made no verbal reply, only sighing deeply and allowing our esteemed local magistrate to draw his own conclusion. He looked very troubled. 'I thought the incident with your brother was the only occasion.'

'Would that that were the case,' I said in an unhappy tone. Tyrone had schooled me. 'But I shall go down and let her in.'

'Is it safe?' he said fearfully. And then he recognized the absurdity of a man afraid of his own daughter. 'I mean, of course you must. I shall see to it that she calms herself.'

I took myself down to the front door. The wind was finding ways through the bricks and it sounded as if the house itself were howling in distress.

She was banging on the door hard enough to beat her way in. It was thick oak, and yet the vehemence of her attack was like to splinter it soon, I thought. I could not understand how she could beat with such force with her bare hands. But I did not have long to wait, because before my sight, it started to splinter. Long cracks appeared and I was stopped in my approach by amazement. And then the tool she was using burst right through: a huge flint she must have pulled from the garden for the task. It had become a hatchet in her grasp. I considered, for a second, whether my life truly was in danger – if her mind had shattered like the door, then James might not be the last of our family to die by her hand.

But I saw Tyrone standing in the entrance to the kitchen and one angry look from him was enough to give me a burst of courage. I moved more quickly to unbar the house to her.

The moment I turned the key in the lock, the wind wrenched the door from me, slamming it against the wall and affording me the first glimpse of the changed Florence.

What a sight she was! Oh, that I could say it did not affect me, but the truth is that it stirred me greatly. Her clothes clung to her, the pink of her skin through the white linen as rosy as if it were open to the air and my eyes. Such waifish, sylvan beauty was never meant to be hidden.

'Lord above, you poor child!' I exclaimed. 'You did not take a latchkey?'

'Why would I take a latchkey?' she demanded. And she threw aside the flint. Droplets of red blood went with it – she had cut open her palm as she beat again and again at the door. She pushed me aside as she bundled into the hallway.

'The servants have been sent home,' I explained.

'You heard me shouting. I was out there for an hour.'

'The storm is very loud.'

'The storm? To Hell with the storm.' She cast aside her outer layer, stripping to her undergarments. 'Stare, don't stare. I don't care what you do!' she declared. And she began to pull away the straps keeping even her skimpy covering in place.

'Florence!' It was shouted from above us. At the top of the flight of stairs, her father was witnessing her apparent attempt to show all of her woman's body to me, her brother-in-law, her divine. 'Stop that! Put your clothes back on! What on earth has entered your head?'

'Oh, good G—d, Father,' she muttered with irritation. 'From a storm to a squall. It's my house, Father, I'll be naked as Eve if I want. You have seen me that way at some point in time, haven't you?' He seemed flustered and stumbled as he tried to descend the staircase. 'Though sometimes I wonder that I was conceived at all. Mother must have been as drunk as you are right now.'

'How dare you!' he cried. And he missed another step, catching at the banister for his life. 'Cover yourself. James's death has distressed us all, but—'

'It hasn't distressed you one hundredth of how it has distressed me,' she hissed. 'You – what? – knew him? Had been in a tavern with him while he bought the drinks and entertained with stories? What's that next to what he was to me? You can leave it behind and find another man to stand the beer and talk about wenches he once knew. I can't. So don't tell me how to mourn my husband's death or how I must behave between my own four walls.'

And she swept up to her chamber. A dirty night, but a pleasing end to it.

21 June 1879

A shock this morning – may the Lord send me fewer in future – as Tyrone stormed into my chamber to shake me out of slumber and inform me that Florence had gone for the morning train to London. I have become concerned with the upstart beginning to develop ideas above his station in life. I must not let him play Cassius to my Caesar.

'Where do you think she's going?' he snarled.

I thought for a second. 'To find Annie White, I presume,' I answered. 'And I agree that it is most disagreeable.'

'So what are we going to do about it?'

'We will follow her to London – not to forestall her, but to beat her to the quarry. We will find Annie and see to it that no inconvenient utterances issue from her lips,' I explained. And I feel that he was impressed by my resolution.

I made the arrangements and soon enough we were waiting for the afternoon train from Colchester to London.

'Good afternoon,' I bade the stationmaster as we stood on the platform. He was from Mersea originally and I knew him a little.

'Afternoon, Parson.'

'I am following my sister-in-law to London. She was supposed to tell me where she was putting up there.'

'Forgot, did she?' he chuckled.

'She did that.'

'Women, Parson. Forget them own names.'

'Quite. So, did she happen to mention it to you? Or anything else that could help me meet her there?'

'No, sir, no.' He shook his head and I set foot on the running plate. 'Oh, but wait! One thing. You see, when she asks me which London station we get into, I tell her it was Liverpool Street.' I presumed there was more of the story to come, but at that point he seemed to find tapping his foul pipe against his heel to loosen the spent tobacco to be of the utmost importance.

'So?' I prompted him.

'So she asks of me,' his mind was still on the pipe, 'how far that is from Covent Garden.' I was pleased by this. Would there be more, perchance? There would. '"Going to see the Punch and Judy box?" I ask her. "No," she says. "Finding someone there." So I tell her that it's twenty minutes by Hackney cab.'

Finding someone there. I thanked the Lord for His Providence.

And yet, oh my! What a journey we had. While I have usually enjoyed my sojourns in the nation's capital, the rickety journey has generally left such an imprint on my body that I have forsworn ever returning. This time was no better.

Finally, we arrived and, upon our stopping at Liverpool Street Station in the early evening, I made my way to the station mail office. I had a stratagem to execute. I found a grubby little man inside and left him instructions and a bank note for a pound.

Thence we made our way to Covent Garden market. We were wary of being seen by Florence before she saw us, so I had changed into common clothing and wore a low-brimmed hat. Tyrone wrapped a black kerchief around the lower portion of his face. It disguised him and made him hardly more noticeable in that den of thieves. Yet if there is one thing that I hate about London, it is the smog, and it was hanging over the whole city, pierced only slightly by the overhead lamps.

So Florence was searching for Annie in Covent Garden. It was clear why such as Annie would be drawn to that place — its night women were legendary from there to Vienna. And they hardly kept their strumpetry to the night. 'Over here, sir!' 'I will make you happy!' Such cheap sin. As Tyrone and I walked, we were subject to a hundred calls and invitations from painted females of all ages — as young as twelve and old as fifty, some of them, I would guess when I came close enough to make them out.

'Later, ladies!' Tyrone called back. 'Be ready, because I have a lot to send your way.' He was rewarded with a cat's choir of sharp laughter. He was quite prepared to descend to their level of pleasures, but first we made a quick sweep of the market and the surrounding alleyways. Neither Annie nor Florence was in sight. That would have been too much to ask for. And so we spent much

of the day on foot, making discreet enquiries. But nothing presented and we retired to a nearby hotel.

22 June 1879

We resumed our search, tramping again for hours before something occurred.

'Are you looking for a woman?' It was not a female voice this time. It was whispered from a doorway, and as I came close in the gloom, I saw a thin man, his face more pockmarked than any I had ever seen — it was a wonder he was still alive, with that series of pits and eruptions on his flesh, and I made certain not to step within breathing distance, lest I catch what he had.

'I am not,' I said, keeping back, waiting to see how he would respond.

His evil-painted face broke into two at that and his voice changed, became somehow knowing of me. 'I know. You are looking for two women. From distant parts.' And without another breath, he disappeared into the shadow of the doorway.

I hesitated, quite unsure about following this man into his lair. 'Go on then,' Tyrone insisted.

'We know nothing of him,' I replied.

Tyrone sneered at me. 'What, are you still a coward?'

'Be quiet!' I snapped at him.

'Don't trouble yourself. I'll go,' he said. 'You wait here.'

His hand went to the bulge beneath his jerkin that I knew to be the knife that had done for Annie's brother. I knew he was itching to use it on the sister too.

On this occasion, I thought it prudent to accede to his suggestion and I went to the other side of the street. 'Up you come, then, sir,' I heard the pander tell my friend as I withdrew.

I remained in the narrow lane, which was just wide enough for one of the fruit or flower carts to trundle along. Its cobbles were wet with moisture, no doubt having been washed through with Thames water to cleanse as much of the daily filth as possible. I looked to the upper storey of the house. A shuttered window showed evidence of a lit candle behind. That would probably be his destination.

There was another girl at the end of the street, standing under a lamp. 'Only three bob, sir!' she called over. 'Lying down. Two upright.'

'Be quiet, whore,' I ordered her.

I waited, beginning to chill, for two minutes at most, before Tyrone came flying out. 'We must leave!' he growled, grabbing my coat and yanking me up the lane.

'What has happened?' I demanded.

'There's no time.' I stared at him. The lamplight was in his eyes as if there were fires behind them. I shook him off and hurried towards the doorway. I would let no man tell me what I could or could not do.

I went quickly up the stairs and into the sole room on the floor above. I was expecting a rough bedroom, a place of work for the pander and his stock beasts, but I found something else. I found a charnel house.

On the bed, their throats torn, were two street geese. They wore the clothes of their trade – sluttishly arranged to show as much skin as possible. They were draped across the cot without care, their blood sprayed not just on the floor, but up the walls too. And neither bore the slightest resemblance to Annie or Florence.

But someone was still alive. 'My, my . . .' I heard someone

groan. The pimp was slumped against a stool. He was stretching a hand to me, while the other seemed to hold his innards, which were spilling from his torso. 'Please . . .' The word turned into a hiss like a snake, which was no doubt appropriate, for surely the Devil himself was there in that room.

'I told you we had to leave.'

This voice I knew. Tyrone had followed me in and stood now behind me.

'What in Heaven's name has got into you?' I demanded.

'Hush your voice.' It was a most stern command. 'I'm in charge in these matters.'

'I . . . water. Surgeon.' The whoremaster was yet alive and moaning. Tyrone's gaze met mine. Then I turned my back and he went to the man on the floor. I heard no more words from that person.

'I'm in charge in these matters,' Tyrone repeated. And there was a very slight rustling, as if he was wiping metal on cloth.

I overlooked the scene again. It would be something to make the penny blood pamphlets. Carnage such as something from the Old Testament. But, of course, that made sense. G—d's hand was in that room, as it was in the Israel of old.

But still. Tyrone had angered me.

'From now on, you do nothing like this!' I declared. 'You overstep what is decent.'

'And that is exactly why you need me!' he countered with the same fury I had exhibited.

'What do you mean?'

'What do I mean?' he said in a mocking tone. 'I mean only what you know: that I have been your sin-eater.'

I stopped, amazed by this assertion. 'How do you even know that term?' I demanded.

'How? Where I grew up, everyone knows it.'

'Well, it is certain that this was sinful,' I said, waving my hand at the bloody scene, not interested in a theological discussion at that moment.

'They sin forty times a day.' He said it utterly dismissively, as if he did not care a jot for these lives. And he prodded the foot of one of the whores with his own. It swung a little, dangling over the edge of the bed. 'Sin always comes around. I am resolved to it.'

'Well, I am not.'

He grinned horribly at that. 'Then maybe you should be.' And there was something in those words that I found quite chilling. 'Now, come on,' he instructed me, grabbing my jacket and this time brooking no refusal. In the doorway, he looked out onto the street, holding the wicked knife in a shadow. 'It's clear,' he said, beckoning me with him. And as we stepped out, he slipped the knife back into a leather scabbard under his tunic. We strode quickly along the lane.

'Want me now, sir?' It was the slut who had enticed me earlier. 'You look ready for it.'

Yet it was not me who replied, but Tyrone. 'I am that,' he said, surprising me. 'Quite ready for it.' And amazing as it was, he made to go to her.

'Are you out of your wits?' I demanded in a whisper and catching hold of him.

'No, just hungry,' he replied with a chuckle. He shook me off and went over to the girl – a younger example of that profession than those lying ripped in the room above us – and without prologue seized her by the shoulders, turned her round, bent her over and went straight at her like a dog in a garden. I looked away, furious at being made a party to this, as well as at the recklessness of the timing.

'There's six bob for you,' I heard him say. 'Treat the girls upstairs to a drink. Courtesy of Dr Black.' He smirked over his shoulder at me.

'Much thanks to you and the doctor, sir,' she replied, her tone quite happy.

I felt his hand on my back, telling me he was ready to leave, and I strode away, pondering how long it would be before I abandoned my erstwhile friend to whatever fate he had waiting for him: the hangman's rope, no doubt.

I took care — more care than he did — to be seen by few people as we returned to the lodging I had engaged near Liverpool Street Station. Tyrone seemed to exult in his recent act and wanted to be seen. 'Let's go to St James's Park. There are more geese there,' he informed me. 'They run about between the hedges, ripe for plucking.' Had he not had his hand on the covered hilt of his knife, I might have given him a stronger admonishment than words alone; but as it was, I called him five different words for a fool and almost dragged him with me back to our hotel. I made sure, though, to take a roundabout path to reduce the chances of our being traced to that establishment and possibly even identified by the Queen's authorities. Tyrone seemed to care nothing if a noose were to wind around his throat, but the prospect was a distinctly unpleasant one to my mind.

When we arrived at the hotel, the owner offered us supper. But when he mentioned that trussed goose was being served, Tyrone burst into laughter and I had to give him a swift kick to stop it.

24 June 1879

For a long while, Tyrone and I searched for our quarry. We tried boarding houses, bagnios and Christian missions. Nothing. All I gained was a deeper anger. He was ready to tear more whores apart in the belief that one of them was harbouring Florence, but I held him back. We would not benefit from the increased attention. And our luck eventually changed.

On the third morning, Tyrone came to me. He had been out all night — I did not want to know where — and had gleaned some information. He told me to wait in the hotel and that night he would bring Florence and the village girl to me. I thanked G—d.

I did as he wished, waiting patiently, but far from bringing the two fugitives, he returned around midnight with a deep wound in his shoulder. I dragged it from him that, despite his assurance, his venture had been far from successful. And from then on, I knew I should not believe a word or promise he uttered. I went to bed angry that night and barely slept.

But thank the Holy One again!

I was woken at perhaps eight o'clock in the morning by the grubby little mail master from Liverpool Street Station. As I admitted him to our chamber, he held a letter in his hand.

'Sir, that matter that we spoke of,' he said, holding it up. 'This morning, this was consigned to the early Colchester train. It is the address you told me to watch for.'

It was indeed addressed to our esteemed Justice of the Peace, Watkins. And I knew his daughter's hand, of course.

'You have done very well,' I said.

'You know, sir,' he said in an innocent tone, 'it is not legal to take letters from Her Majesty's mail.'

I sighed. 'The other gentleman will pay you.'

'Other gentleman?' the idiot echoed, peering around him.

I was in no mood for such folly and drew my pocket book from under the pillow, doling out six shillings. It briefly occurred to me that that was the sum Tyrone had given the streetwalker the other night.

'You may leave us,' I said.

'Yes, Father.' He seemed somehow confused by the simple words. I dislike it when rough men I know not address me as 'Father'. It smacks of my having a spiritual or even pastoral duty towards them when I have none.

I opened the packet.

'Florence?' Tyrone enquired.

'For certain.'

I read it thoroughly. It described what had happened to her across the previous three days. It was an amusing read. And there was something far more important about it: it was composed upon hotel notepaper.

And so, I had her address without the slightest trouble: The Crown Hotel, Bishopsgate.

Chapter 17

Simeon looked up from the pages before him and took some time to think over what he had read, what he had learned about this unassuming country parson. Into his mind slipped the memory of Watkins telling him that Oliver Hawes had been cashiered from the army for cowardice and desertion. He wondered if the new psychologists could take that humiliation and connect the links to the man he had become. But there would be time anon for such supposition; now he only needed more information. 'He writes that your letter to your father told him what you had been through in London, but does not include the details. Will you tell me?' he asked.

'I don't enjoy thinking about it.'

'I can understand that. I can't know what it was, but it must have been foul.' She nodded. 'Can I offer you something else, something that would make you happy?'

'Such as?'

'Perhaps you can suggest something.'

She looked thoughtful. 'What's happened to Oliver's body?' she asked.

'It's currently in the morgue at Colchester Royal Hospital.'

'You'll have it interred in the family crypt?'

'I presumed that I would,' he replied, and as he spoke the words, he saw the direction her mind was moving. 'Do you have another idea?'

'I have. I want you to put John White in his place. He deserves a decent interment.'

It was a striking demand. At first, Simeon thought it impossible, but then, as he considered, it would not be so hard to accomplish. He would oversee the oysterman's body being placed in a coffin and would accompany that casket to the crypt. No one but he would know who was in it. White would otherwise be cast into a pauper's grave.

'And what about Oliver's body?'

The flame-light glinted on her yellow silk. It was as if she were in the fire itself. 'Bury him in the mudflats where you found John. Let him sink. And weigh him down so no one ever finds him.'

Watkins covered his ears.

There was a certain balancing justice to her plan. And what more could he offer but balance? 'I will,' he said.

There was silence for a while. 'Will you now tell me what happened to you?'

'Do you have time to listen?'

'I have all the time in the world.'

He sat on the parson's seat, in silent expectation.

'That accusing note from Annie, the one that Oliver sent to the house to make it look as if she were accusing James of abusing her, not Oliver,' she said, almost to herself, remembering. 'Well, it seemed to me afterwards a very queer coincidence that, at the same time as it arrived, her brother should have an accident, and the next day she should attempt suicide. So I went to visit her, to discover what had happened.'

'I see.'

'I found Annie quite ill, of course, and she said little, but what she said made me suspicious that I had been unfair to James by accusing him on the basis of that note of an involvement with her. But she was keeping much to herself. So when I heard that she had recovered and taken the first train that she could to London, I knew I had to go too.' She poured herself a little water from a jug. 'First off, I decided to throw any pursuers off my scent. Oh, I was a wily fox, Simeon. I asked myself, where would a girl like Annie possibly end up in London? Well, it's sadly obvious, isn't it? If you're a young woman thrown out or without a family to support you, you end up on the streets and in the only profession that doesn't ask for experience. So I put it about that I was heading for Covent Garden, where a good number of these poor women ply their trade. Anyone following me would guess that I had information about her being there.'

'Very subtle of you.'

'It was. But in truth, I had no idea of where she was. Yes, she might well be on the streets – but what about Whitechapel or Camden or Mayfair? The locations where that business goes on are endless. So instead, I planned a search, aided by some money I took from James's strongbox. As a first step, I called in at an emporium where I made a purchase that you men wouldn't approve of.'

'Are you sure we wouldn't?'

'Quite sure.' But then she relented a little. 'In most cases. Well, we'll soon see.' She stopped for a moment. 'The owner of that emporium also recommended the services of a man operating from an office in a backstreet of Soho. It was above a tobacconist's shop and between the fumes from that place and the general fug of London, I thought I was going to pass out at any second. The name of the man who operated from there was Mr Nathaniel Brent. "I have no idea of my true surname. I was found in Brent and they gave me that name, since it was as good as any," he told me.' She reproduced his accent as if she were the roughest guttersnipe in London.

'And who is this Mr Brent?'

'Mr Brent – or any other surname you want to give him – described himself as "an agent of enquiries". In essence, if you want someone tracked like a wounded stag, he's your man. He's of the thin sort, tall. Somehow overbearing. I told him I wished to find a former servant of mine whom I thought had got herself into trouble. The usual sort of trouble.

'He sat down in a chair of his – the only seating in the

whole room, leaving me standing, which I thought a bit off. And he spoke. "Funny thing is, miss, 'most everyone who comes through that door tells me one story, then it turns out the truth is something quite different." I flushed a bit, which made me angry at myself. "So, how 'bout you tell me the real reason you want to find this Annie White, and we both pretend it was the first tale you came in with?"' Simeon's mouth creased in amusement. 'Well, I was annoyed, but at least he had proved some wits. I told him the truth. "Devil of a story," he said, though I think it was to himself rather than me. "Poor floozy. Right. Go to your lodging. I'll come with what I can find out. I'll come by the name of Mr Cooryan. Anyone else comes a-calling for you, start screaming the place down. Remember: Mr Cooryan."

'"If someone uninvited comes calling, I shall use this, not my screaming voice," I said. And I opened my clutch bag to show him what I had bought at the emporium that afternoon. It was a rather pretty little four-shot muff pistol, you see. Snug little thing that fits entirely in my hand-warmer. You wouldn't know it was there until you got a bullet or two through the brain.' She fixed Simeon with her gaze. 'So now, what do you think of that?'

'A necessity of modern life,' he said with a shrug, presuming she was hoping for a sharper reaction.

'Ah, yes.' And she inclined her head a little to address Watkins. 'Sorry, Father, I know you brought me up to sew samplers, but times change, don't they?'

Watkins attempted a reply, but failed and sank back into himself.

213

'Anyway, at that I returned to my boarding house and waited. Do you know, Simeon, there's an army living on the streets of London, should any man or woman require them. For a small price, they will fan across the city asking at hospitals, inns and servants' entrances for any name or description that you give them. Most of what they hear will be bunkum, but eventually one will come back with the truth.'

'I was not so aware, no,' he said.

'But it's true. And a few days later, Nathaniel brought me what I was looking for. It was an address in St George's Fields in Southwark.'

St George's Fields. He understood immediately. Yes, he had seen that place himself and had sympathy for any who resided there. 'I can guess the address you mean.'

'I thought you might. Well, Nathaniel asked me if I knew about these places. I told him that I had read about them, but never thought I would be visiting one. "No, miss, not many do."

'And yet, the very next day, I was in a Hansom heading for it.'

Simeon interrupted. 'The Magdalen Hospital for the Reception of Penitent Prostitutes,' he said. 'You don't forget that name.'

'You don't. So, there I was before this large brick building that looked much like a prison.' In her glass cell, she ran her hand along the front of that edifice. 'Have you ever been inside?'

'No. But my brother medics have told me strong stories.'

She nodded in understanding. 'It's all locked and

214

barred, with wooden blinds over the windows so that no one can see in. That's to stop the inmates from plying their trade from the hospital itself.'

'I've heard so.'

'Men get some sort of thrill from looking at fallen women, it seems. I wondered about James then, if he would have had that thrill.' She gently shook her head. 'But I'm getting away from the point. I marched up to the gate and spun them some story about wanting to contribute to the asylum, but requiring a tour of it first. I did my best to sound like you, Father, when you have a prisoner in the dock. Imperious. Puffed up.'

Here, Watkins summoned up his last vestiges of dignity. 'It is the law, Florence. It must be respected!'

And she lost her temper in full for the first time that Simeon had known. 'The law? Hah!' she shouted, striking the glass with her palm. 'It's your law that put me in here! Your law that means I'll never be allowed out. Isn't that right? Whether I'm behind this for madness or murder, it makes no odds, does it? I'm still here. And I'll be here until I die!'

Watkins rubbed his eyes. 'I am sorry, my girl,' he said. 'I was tricked.'

'You weren't the only one, sir,' Simeon informed him, trying to cool the waters. 'There's a long line before and after you.'

Watkins accepted the words with thanks and they watched Florence's chest heave with suppressed passion. She whirled away from them and it was a while before she came back, a colder anger in her eyes.

'I'll return to the story. But we'll speak, Father. We will speak.' Watkins met Simeon's gaze. 'A thin, grasping woman warden – I could tell she was looking to line her own pocket – obliged my request and I asked her a few questions which she was happy to answer. Did you know that one in three of the inmates is under the age of thirteen?'

'It's sickening,' Simeon agreed. 'Worst of all is that there's little we can do about it. Their families have no choice: it's that or starvation.'

'Hmm. Well. I steered the conversation to punishment of those inmates who were not wholly repentant. The woman looked at me shiftily. I wasn't supposed to ask about that. "There is Heaven and there is Hell. God has rewards and punishments, we his instruments must have too," I said. She told me about some minor mistreatments – reduced food, no permission to talk, work hours increased from fourteen to sixteen hours per day turning the mangle in the laundry. "That all sounds paltry," I said. "That won't change a wanton mind." And I said something dark about subscribing my money elsewhere. She looked panicked and told me of something they called "the hard room". And I knew she hadn't wanted to, because I had been told by Nathaniel Brent that that was where I had to look. "What is that?" I asked.

'"Where the really awful women go. Those that refuse to do their work or such. They're given cold baths and stay there in isolation. We only use it on those that can't leave the asylum."

'"Why can't they leave?"

'"Different reasons," she told me. "There's one there now that was caught robbing her customer. She pleaded so much that the judge said he would stay the rope if she came here and repented before God."

'"A very forward-thinking judge."

'"Yes, madam."

'"Why is she refusing to work?"

'"Can't say. She's not dying. Those that are dying, we put out on the street."

'She said that, you know, with utter callousness.' Simeon was not in the least surprised. '"I wish to see it. I wish to question her and make sure that her repentance is real," I told her. Well, she tried to brush me off, of course, but I insisted and she gave up and took me. After winding through the building, we came to an iron door at the end of a long passage. I could hear a strange sound as we came close. It was not speech or sobbing exactly. And then, when she unlocked the door, to my horror I saw what it was. There was Annie, utterly unclothed on the floor, huddling herself, and her teeth chattering so much that the whine coming from her mouth was being chopped up into short notes like some sort of mad songbird.

'"Cold baths," the warden said. God help me, she was proud of it. "Have her working soon. On the mangle." Then she spoke to Annie loudly and slowly, like you talk to a child. "We'll soon have you working. Unless you want Tyburn."

'At that, Annie looked up for the first time. It took her a few seconds to recognize me, but then she just looked amazed. She made an effort to speak, but she couldn't. I think it wasn't just that her teeth were chattering so, it was having lived a month that had seen her attempt her own death, her brother gone, her flight to London, her arrest as a streetwalker and thief and her incarceration in this brutal place. Who could have remained strong in mind and body after all that?' Florence stared off to the side of her cell before returning to the story. '"I am taking her," I said, and I knelt to the girl and spoke to her as gently as I could. "Home. Annie, we're going home."

'"I don't understand," the warden said. "What?"

'"I am taking her back to her mother. Unless you want me to write to everyone from the trial judge to the Archbishop of Canterbury to tell them how you are abusing the trust they put in you, you are going to collect her clothes and give them to me, and I am taking her home."' Florence grinned at the memory and the smile flitted to Simeon's mouth.

'Well, that put the wind up her. And within ten minutes, we were out the front gate.' She gazed up at the line of windows in the library, as if she could look through them all the way to London. 'We sat in St George's Fields, within sight of the asylum, but with our backs to it. She was too exhausted to go any further. "Annie," I said. "I'll take you home." But all she could do was look at me. And we stayed there for an hour or more, not speaking. I bought some small beer and pies from a hawker, and she ate so quickly I thought she would be ill, but it seemed to bring her back a little. And then, finally, she was able to stand and walk with me. God, how I wish that had been the end of our troubles.'

'Something tells me they were only just beginning,' Simeon replied.

'How perceptive you are. Well, as we went along the street, with Annie shivering even though it was a warm night, I saw a man on the other side of the road. He was dressed in black, with a big hat pulled down and his face covered with a scarf. If I had ever known him, I couldn't recognize him then. But I had no reason to pay him any attention. So Annie and I set off up the street towards the Thames, where we could cross by way of the new bridge. I couldn't help but look back at the asylum, though, horrible place that it is. And as I did that, I saw the man in black was still behind us, keeping pace. All my instincts told me to get away as soon as I could, so I took Annie's arm and hurried off.

'Over my shoulder, I saw he had stopped and was looking back the way he had come, which was strange. Then he raised his arm, and suddenly a carriage sped along the road towards us. The driver must have been desperate for his own death, though, the rate he was moving. As it passed, the man on foot leaped onto the running board and hung there as it bore down on us. I can't tell you how frightening that sight was.'

'I'm sure.'

'I shouted to Annie to run and we made a break for an alley opposite. If she had been well and healthy, I think we would have made it. But she was so weak, she was like a fetter to me. And then the coach was a yard away and the man in black threw himself upon us both, knocking us to the ground.' She broke off for a moment, breathing heavily, before composing herself to resume her story. 'He kicked Annie hard, knocking her unconscious, I think. The driver, a fair-haired lump, jumped off the coach, straight onto me, knocking the wind out of me, and I felt him tying my hands behind my back and pulling a hood over my head.' Simeon felt a bolt of anger at the image, a man trussing her like game.

'I heard the one in black shout, "Get these bitches into the carriage." And I was lifted up and thrown in. "Stay down and you won't get hurt."

'I'd like to say I was brave and defiant, Simeon, but really I was scared out of my wits. I asked who they were. "Don't matter to you," was the only answer I got. And then I felt something cold on the back of my neck. It was the edge of a blade and I tried to press myself away from it, into the floor of the carriage, even though we were bumping up and down, galloping towards . . . somewhere. The man was bellowing, "Faster, for God's sake! Faster!" and I heard him thumping at the roof. I think my teeth nearly broke against the floor. "Now stop!" he said. And we came to a sudden halt. I could hear birds. Maybe the river, but that was probably my imagination. "All right, what will you bid me for this one?" I thought we were to be sold. I was as terrified as you can imagine. Would we be locked away? Sent overseas? Killed? But then I understood, because the one with the covered face whispered in my ear. "Well, Mrs Hawes?" he said. "What do you think you're worth?"'

'So they were after you,' Simeon said.

'Yes, they were. And it frightened me five hells more

than if they had just picked up two easy females from the street. "No, no easy life for you on your back," he said. I think he thought it very witty. I told him I could get him money. "My father is wealthy. And he is a magistrate, so the law won't forget me," I said.

'"A magistrate, you say? Oh, I know that, Mrs Hawes. A drunken JP. Who would care about him?"' Florence's gaze shifted to address her father. 'I wondered if he did know you, Father.'

'Oh, Florence,' he groaned.

She dismissed his words with a waft of her hand. '*Oh, Florence* nothing. I told him you were a man with friends. "Friends? Watkins? Ha!" was his only reply. Well, his contempt doubled my fear. He obviously didn't care about the law or retribution, so I pictured all sorts of suffering ahead of us. I had time to do it, too. We waited there for what felt like hours and I have no idea what happened in that time or what we were waiting for, but I heard distant sounds – a coach rumbling by, dogs barking. Time is like a weight upon you when it's all you have, you know. I learned that in that coach and in this cell.' She stared at her father. 'Well, eventually the man spoke again. "Mrs Hawes, I'm ready for you now."

'"Please," I said.

'"Beg all you want. I like it." Yes, it looked like it was all over.'

'It can't have been,' Simeon said.

'No. Just as I thought our fate was sealed, everything turned again.'

'How so?'

'Because as I lay there, trussed, unable to breathe with fear, there came the most ear-splitting explosion I have ever heard. It was as if the carriage itself had blown apart.' She paused, allowing them to guess. 'Screaming, someone in terrible pain. My heart was in my mouth and I couldn't see what was happening. Yelling as best I could, I tried to get my hands free, but they were tied tight.' Simeon felt his pulse beat faster. 'Then I felt the point of a dagger – the one I had felt against my neck, I presumed – stabbing into my wrists. "Please, no!" I called out and I felt blood running down my wrists. But there was a different voice to the one I was expecting. "It's all right, Mrs Hawes, it's all right. It's me. Annie." And the ropes around my wrists burst apart. Annie pulled the hood off my face and I could see the floor of the carriage. And to the side was the face of the lumpen blond man who had jumped on me.' The edge of her lips curled up in cruelty. 'I say his face was there, but half of it was gone. And I saw the four-shot pistol I had kept in my hand-warmer. It was in Annie's hand and had been fired.'

Chapter 18

Simeon met her gaze. 'Its purchase stood you well.'

Her eyes glittered. 'I've seen foxes torn apart and it doesn't bother me to see them. I didn't care a jot for this man, whose face had been ripped apart and thrown over one shoulder. Annie finally cut through the other ropes and I saw that the carriage only contained me, her and the dead man.'

'Quite the reversal of fortune,' Simeon said.

'"Where's the other one?" I asked Annie. "Did you get him too?"

'"No, he ran." She pointed out the open door. I looked outside. It was dark and we were on an empty stretch of scrub ground by the Thames. I couldn't see him anywhere.

223

I asked her how she was. "Better, Mrs Hawes. Who was that?" I said I didn't know. You see, I had to work it out, and I knew then, from what that man with the masked face had said, that it all hinged on what had happened here on Ray. So I had to know the truth. "Annie," I said. "People are saying it was my husband who ... brought you low." She looked at me quite blankly. "Was it James?"

'She shook her head. "No, Mrs Hawes," she said. "No, not him. It were the parson done it." And that's how I knew. That's how I realized Oliver was her abuser and John's murderer.

'"Annie," I said. "We need to ..." but even before I could finish, she grabbed my shoulder. "There!" she shouted. I spun around. The man with the black scarf was pulling open the door on the other side of the coach. It wasn't over yet. I grabbed the pistol from her, levelled it and drew the trigger. Oh, that sound.' She smiled. 'It shattered my ears and the gun kicked back, right out of my grip, you know. But through the barrel smoke, I could see I had hit his shoulder – his shirt was tattered and wet with his blood. But I knew he wasn't finished, because his eyes, which were still all I could see of him, met mine and narrowed. And he threw open the door.'

'The man felt no pain, by the sound of it,' Simeon said.

'He showed no sign. He just yelled, "Come here!" and pulled himself up, but I got hold of the pistol and fired again. This time, he dodged the bullet. Annie was screaming. But he came back to the door and I knew this time I had to be true with my shot. So I breathed, imagined the gun was part of my hand and stretched it towards him. It was pointing dead at his heart. "This time I won't miss," I spat at him. And his eyes bore into mine. He knew I was telling the truth and I began squeezing back on the trigger. But at the last moment, he threw himself backwards, out of the carriage. I held my finger. It was my last bullet and I needed it.'

'What then?'

'I heard his footsteps running away. I gave it a few seconds, then checked outside. I couldn't see him, so I crept out with the pistol raised. Suddenly, he darted out from under the carriage and snatched for me, but I pulled away and scrambled up to the coach driver's seat. He was getting to his feet so I grabbed the reins, the horses leaped forward and we were gone.' Her hands lifted in the air as if in exultation.

'Florence,' was all Simeon could say, struck to the quick by the narrative.

'A triumph, yes.' But then a graver air descended on her. 'But it did not last.'

'How so?'

She paused for a moment. 'It would be better if you read the rest of Oliver's journal.'

He looked down. He had quite forgotten the loose pages in his hand, rapt as he had been in the live remembrance before him.

'Need we read every word?' Watkins burst out. 'The man was a murderer. Must you honour him by reading his thoughts?'

'I think I must, Mr Watkins,' Simeon replied. 'The truth will out.'

The magistrate moaned once more and dropped his hands in submission. 'Then do it. Though I for one would rather cast that book into the fire.'

'Maybe I'll do that afterwards.'

There were only a few pages left unread, continuing from the point where Hawes had intercepted Florence's letter to her father, so gaining the name of her hotel in London.

And so, I had her address without the slightest trouble: The Crown Hotel, Bishopsgate. 'Father. As you can see, I am currently in an hotel in London for reasons I am about to reveal to you,' her missive ran. There then followed a detailed description of her previous few days' exertions. Such a waste of effort, for I would see to it that Watkins was never troubled by the letter's contents.

And yet Tyrone had seemingly attempted and failed to take her by force the previous night. If I could not take hold of her and the village girl whom Tyrone had enjoyed, what could I do about them? The answer, I decided, was to allow the keepers of the Queen's Peace to step in.

The police magistrate for that parish was a very old fellow who should probably have retired many years earlier, but it was a thankless task with a low sinecure, so the Home Secretary would have been hard-pressed to find anyone else willing to take it on. I went to him with the necessary information: my sister-in-law, who was known to have killed my brother in a wild temper, had absconded to London, where she had, very strangely, removed a convicted prostitute from the Magdalen asylum. I, her parson as well as her brother-in-law, had been commissioned by her father, the local Justice of the Peace, to return her home, where she would face justice and kindness in equal measure. I would also take the prostitute, since she was of our parish, thus removing one more disease-spreader from the police magistrate's books.

All of this was entirely true and bore no false witness, so I was pleased with the course of action.

It stands as a testament to the Sodomish nature of the capital that all I said hardly raised an eyebrow, and the man instead made an immediate order that a pair of constables were to accompany me to The Crown Hotel in Bishopsgate to retrieve the runaways. He would also write to Watkins, to warn him of his daughter's mental instability and explain that she was now in my care, so he need not worry.

I thanked him and made my way back to my lodging. On the way, Tyrone called in at some dreadful establishment near the docks. He came out with a bottle of strong laudanum, a funnel and a rubber tube, insisting that they would come in useful.

Thank the Lord for the English policing forces! These men knew their game, all right — which is why, barely four hours later, our two cats were being dragged towards the Colchester train, spitting and hissing enough to make me think twice whether I would be able to stand the journey.

'I'll cut your throat, you son of a whore!' You might have thought it would be the common girl screeching such things, rather than the daughter of a magistrate, but you would be mistaken. It was Florence who was shouting such oaths as to make Lucifer turn tail. But no matter, I had come armed for such a show of defiance. The loyal constables aided me by holding her still while I forced the funnel and tube down her throat and dosed her with the laudanum. Wonderful stuff! It was a minute, no more, before she was like a rag doll. The other harlot was less trouble, accepting her drink without struggle. I think she enjoyed it. They were obedient as dozing lambs from then on.

I had reserved a small compartment. The guard seemed a little perturbed by our party, but my garb of office and the presence of the constables reassured him that all was 'ship-shape' as he said.

And so, the police left us and we set off. It was a predictably tedious few hours to Colchester, where we hired a trap which, at Tyrone's request, set us down on a lonely stretch of road close to the Peldon Rose. I asked him why he wanted to dismiss it there. He pointed at the village girl. 'I want to enjoy her one last time. What does it matter to you?'

'If you must,' I said. 'I'll give Florence another dose.'

'A good idea.'

I stood waiting by the roadside while he carried the girl into a copse of trees. Florence was at my feet. He was gone thirty minutes, and I began to worry that we would attract attention. In the end, I left our baggage where it lay and hauled Florence half-sensible after Tyrone. 'For Heaven's sake,' I cried at his back when I could make it out in the dark. 'We must go.' But as I came close, I noticed I could not see the girl. 'Where is she?' I asked.

'We don't need her any more,' he said, taking me by the arm and guiding me back towards the road. 'She's comforting her brother.' He grinned. 'Probably the only way she knows how.'

Well, it was true that we were lighter without her, and when I came to think on it, the police magistrate's letter to Watkins – which should have arrived by then – made no mention of us bringing the village girl, so no one was expecting her. Yes, Tyrone had done right again, although whether that was his intention is questionable.

When we arrived home, I sent for Watkins and related how Florence had been arrested. Taken with her assault on James, her mental state was clearly fragile. He begged me to look after her and I agreed, saying that she had been quiet while in my company, thanks to the wonderful medicine in my possession. All this time, she was barely awake. Once or twice she attempted speech but failed to enunciate a syllable. I told Watkins I would arrange good medical supervision. And she would stay in the house.

And so, that night, Florence and I sat gazing at each other in the library. 'I shall have something constructed for you,' I told her. And I stroked her head and I am certain that, at last, she liked it. 'Somewhere for you to live.' I gave her more of the laudanum and she drank it well, and as she lay her head down to sleep she had a look of pure contentment that I swear before Our Father she had never had before.

Chapter 19

There, Simeon left off reading. He looked up at Florence.

'He read me his journal,' she said. 'Every night. When he reached the end, he would start again from the beginning. He always lingered over the passage where he described the delivery of the note from Annie that tricked me to violence. It was Oliver's lie that cut James's cheek, so that his blood was poisoned and he died in my arms. Oliver enjoyed watching me helpless, knowing what he had done to us.'

'Mental pain is the worst of all,' Simeon said, with sympathy. 'I cannot imagine.'

'They say that with time, you get used to anything.'

'They do.'

'But "they" lie, Simeon. Each night, I had to listen to

him crow over my suffering and how he had stolen James's life from him.' Her very complexion seemed to darken. 'Each night, I felt fire – actual fire – in my blood. Some nights, I was strong enough to cast oaths at him, but the next day he would increase the dosage of the laudanum. If I didn't drink it, I would drink nothing. The thirst forced me to take it. But I could still hate. And do you know what happened over time?'

That was obvious. 'I imagine you became immune to the laudanum.'

'Precisely. My thoughts became clearer, my intentions sharper. But I didn't let on. I didn't let him know that I was returning to myself.'

'You were wise.'

'And yet you understood, didn't you, Simeon?'

He nodded. 'It took me time to realize. The first time I saw this glass,' he touched the panel that separated them, it was cold to his skin, 'I saw my own reflection in it, my twin. But in time, I understood that I hadn't been the only man in the room with a double.'

'When did that realization come?'

'When I went to the Red Lantern, at your direction. I think you sent me there because you wanted me to understand the nature of Oliver Hawes's relationship with Mr Tyrone. It worked.'

'He mentioned that den in his cups from time to time.' There was a blaze in her eyes. She was savouring the moment.

He pulled from his jacket the sheet of paper with a man's portrait drawn in violet ink. 'A picture of Tyrone,

231

drawn by the owner of that place. She doesn't want to see him again.'

'Ah.' Florence gazed at the paper, at the ink that stained it. 'She has talent.'

He had to agree. Looking into the rendered eyes, he saw all that that woman and all the others who had met him had seen of this hard subject. 'It's strange how a picture can capture the essence of a man,' he said. 'You can see right into his soul. She said he was hollow. I think that's true.'

'Yes,' Florence said. 'It's quite true.'

He walked to the cold grate and threw the picture in, tossing a lit match after it without another thought. 'And it was at the Red Lantern that I understood how you killed Oliver.'

'Oh, don't stop now, Simeon,' she laughed. 'More, please.'

'As you wish. You killed him not by poisoning him, but by depriving him of poison.' She smiled from ear to ear. 'And he never knew a thing of it. Isn't that right?'

'What?' Watkins asked, in utter confusion.

'Tincture of laudanum,' she asked her father happily, 'do you know what exactly it contains?'

Simeon informed him. 'The normal recipe includes brandy, opium, acetic acid.' He knew where she was leading, but he allowed her the moment of joy.

'That's correct. And you know how it is administered,' she prompted.

'Drunk. Warm or cold.'

'But . . .'

'But one must stir the bottle hard. Yes, I was reminded of that fact when I went to the opium house.'

'So, you do see,' she said approvingly.

'I do.' He spoke to Watkins, explaining what the old man did not understand, without taking his gaze from Florence. 'You stir it because the opium sinks to the bottom of the bottle. Otherwise, the upper drink is pure brandy and the dregs are pure opium.' His eyes explored her face, her cheek, her chin. 'A year ago, while he was still allowing you to sit with him in this room, you poured a bottle of laudanum into his brandy.' She took in a deep breath, as if drinking in the old day. 'It would make no difference at first, but because he ladled the spirit from the top of the barrel, and the opium was at the bottom, as he drank his way through it he was receiving higher and higher doses.'

Her expression took on a faraway look. He knew she was exhilarated by the memory. 'He had dropped his spectacles,' she said, her voice drifting through the creeks. 'He was quite blind without them, so he was hunting about on the floor for, oh, ten or twenty seconds. I poured in the laudanum he used to dose me, gave it a moment to disperse, then refilled the bottle from the keg.' She chuckled to herself. 'But there would be hardly any opium in my bottle.'

'And by the end of the barrel, he was drinking pure poppy,' Simeon added, picturing the man ladling out his drink. 'He must have had a raging addiction without even knowing it.'

'He must.'

'And then, at the end of last month, he finished the barrel and overnight his supply was cut off. The burning in his joints, the vomiting – they were his body crying out for the drug.'

'But there was none to be had.'

'But there was none to be had,' he echoed. 'It might not have killed him, it might have just wracked him with tremendous pain. But in the end his heart gave out. And there will never be the slightest proof that anything unnatural happened.'

There was silence for a while. 'A woman sits here day and night,' Florence said to him. 'She has time for thoughts. For ideas, Simeon.' The lightest of smiles drifted along her lips. 'So much time for ideas.'

THE END